SKINZZ

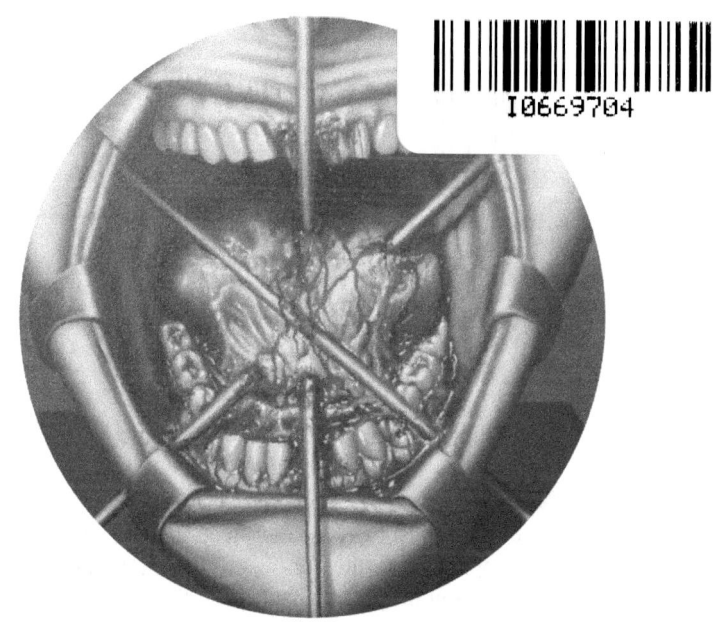

WRATH
JAMES WHITE

deadite
press

DEADITE PRESS
P.O. BOX 10065
PORTLAND, OR 97296
www.DEADITEPRESS.com

AN ERASERHEAD PRESS COMPANY
www.ERASERHEADPRESS.com

ISBN: 978-1-62105-188-6

Printed in the USA.

To Mom

PROLOGUE

Philadelphia, December 15, 1988, Club Pizazz

Miranda was one tough bitch. That's how she would have referred to herself and that's how Mack thought of her. One tough bitch. Most guys said she was too manly to be pretty. Her jaw a little too square, nose a little too aquiline, shoulders a little too broad, body a little too lean and wiry. But Mack thought she was perfect. Her skin was that flawless porcelain white that Goth chicks spent tons of makeup and half an hour in the mirror trying to duplicate. There was not a blemish on it except for the occasional bruise or cut after a fight. To him, she looked like a Greek goddess.

Most people assumed Miranda was a lesbian. With her short spiky black hair and her disdain for skirts or makeup, it was an easy mistake to make. Typically, she wore black jeans, black police-issue equestrian boots, a white t-shirt beneath a flannel, topped with a black motorcycle jacket. She wore a spiked dog collar around her neck and a spiked wristband. She smoked cigarettes in aggressive motions as if Andrew Dice Clay taught her the habit. There was an androgynousness about her that Mack found extremely sexy. He was pretty sure that she was bi. He'd seen her hanging out at a lesbian bar on Spruce Street called Maude's and saw her kiss a girl once. It was probably the sexiest thing he'd ever seen. He kissed her once himself, the first night he hung out with the group of punk rockers he now called family. It was also his first night getting drunk and the first time he ever kissed a girl who smoked. He'd found the taste of beer and cigarettes arousing. He could still remember the taste

5

now when he closed his eyes. Mack could remember the feel of her lips, her tongue, her hard body pressed against his. Nothing else ever came of the kiss and it was never repeated, but Mack still cherished it, just as he cherished her.

She nodded to him and smiled as she walked past. He nodded back, smiling awkwardly, wanting so bad to talk to her but feeling clumsy and nervous, not knowing what to say. Miranda was the only girl in the scene he gave two shits about, except maybe for Alexis and he just wanted to fuck her because she had the biggest titties he'd ever seen. He was pretty sure he was in love with Miranda. He came to the shows as much to see her as he did to kick skinhead ass.

A large group of skinheads congregated in the back of the club, jeering and threatening everyone who passed them. They were starting early, setting the tone for the night. Several punks flipped them the bird or grabbed their crotch as they passed. A guy with three short black and pink Mohawks, mooned the group of skinheads before flipping both middle fingers at them. Several skins had to be restrained by their friends to keep from attacking and getting them all thrown out before the concert was in full swing.

Miranda passed them several times, clearly itching for a fight. She had a tooth missing in the front from the last big skinhead brawl at City Gardens in New Jersey. She was apparently looking for payback. Mack didn't think the missing tooth detracted from her beauty one bit. If anything, it accentuated it in his mind. He often said that he wanted a girl with scars on her knuckles and Miranda was that girl. To Mack, there was something kick ass about a woman who kicked ass and Miranda hated skinheads almost as much as he did.

The club had been open for less than an hour. Already there were more than twenty of the baldheaded Nazi bastards and their numbers seemed to be increasing every minute. Mack looked around at the smattering of punks scattered throughout the club, hoping the number of punks continued to grow in order to maintain the balance of power. He was certain that if the skinhead's ranks exceeded that of the punks they'd attack immediately.

The skinheads were dressed almost identically in green bomber jackets, Levis, white t-shirts or thermals, and oxblood Doc Martin combat boots. Their heads glowed like Halloween skulls beneath the strobe lights in the dimly lit nightclub. Some had swastikas tattooed on their arms, hands, some even had them on their heads or necks and one had a tattoo on his cheek. They were members of a white power group from New Jersey called *The Unrest* and, unlike a lot of other skinheads who tried to hide their hatred and bigotry, they wore theirs proudly.

Mack was not a small kid. He was over six feet. His arms, shoulders, and chest were heavily muscled even though he had a small waist and skinny legs. He had seen many skinheads stammer and stutter when he confronted them, claiming that they promoted "White Pride" not "White Power" and that they didn't hate anyone. They said they were just celebrating their heritage the way other races and nationalities were free to celebrate theirs. Mack always thought that was bullshit and had grudging respect for *The Unrest* for not hiding behind such cowardly rationalizations. Still, he hated every one of them and would happily kill them all if given half a chance. His grandparents and great grandparents had marched for civil rights. His grandmother could vividly recall being told to use the colored bathrooms and being evicted from an all-white pool. His great uncle had been beaten by cops and arrested during a civil rights march on Washington. The idea that these assholes were trying to turn back the clock and rescind the equality that so many had suffered and died for enraged Mack.

The Unrest began as a hardcore band fronted by a skinhead named John Jones. The group sucked, but their inflammatory, racist lyrics garnered them a following anyway despite their lack of genuine musical talent. After fights began breaking out at all of their concerts, they were banned from just about every music venue on the east coast. That's when they went from being a band to becoming a movement. Now, *The Unrest* was one of the most violent and vocal neo-Nazi skinhead organizations in the Tri-state area.

The skinheads stared at Mack with undisguised disdain. Mack knew they would have already lynched him if they could have, but Mack wasn't just black, he was big, he could fight like the devil, and he was popular. He knew half the kids in the club would rush to his aid if it came down to a fight. It was looking like he was going to get a chance to test that theory.

Mack came to Club Pizazz looking to kick some skinhead ass and so had most of the punks in the place, including Miranda. Alexis and Breezy were there too, but they had probably come to actually hear the bands. Those chicks went to every concert, regardless of who was playing. *Uncivil Disobedience* was headlining along with *Terrorist Threat* and everyone knew that a group like *Uncivil Disobedience* would bring all the bald Nazi bastards streaming out of the suburbs and across and through every bridge and tunnel. Kids who never showed up for shows and didn't even like hardcore music came out just for the opportunity to bash the Nazi motherfuckers.

The bouncers would be busy tonight. They frisked everyone who walked in and waved metal detection wands up and down their bodies. It only made Mack slightly more at ease. He had a knife in one boot and a pair of brass knuckles in the other. If he could sneak weapons in, so could they.

Mack could feel the adrenalin seeping into his bloodstream. His muscles tensed. His heart rate increased, preparing for a fight. The air was charged with violence like someone had turned on an electric generator. Mack could almost see the current traveling from person to person. At its center, was the ever-growing group of white supremacists. There were almost a hundred of them. This was going to be one hell of a fight. Mack kept one eye on them as he bounced up and down to the frantic drums and guitar of *Terrorist Threat*. The lead singer belted out lyrics as if they were being sprayed from a submachine gun.

"Violence and Pain!
Violence and Pain!
I love this world!
Of violence and pain!
Life is so cruel!
Love is so violent!
Drain the gene pool
Nonviolence is silence!"

The crowd seethed. Roiling waves of humanity crashed against one another as the pit went wild. Beside him, Mack's best friend Jason was doing a frenetic pogo, bouncing up and down and slamming into the other dancers. Soon, the pit resembled a riot. Mack tried to keep his eyes on the skinheads as they moved toward the pit, pushing and shoving their way through the crowd. One of them knocked over a small Asian Goth chick. One of the other skinheads kicked the girl while she was down. Miranda came out of nowhere and punched the skinhead who'd knocked the girl down, catching him square in the mouth and staggering him. She threw three more punches that shattered the guy's nose, busted his lip and dropped him on his ass. Another skinhead stepped forward and she didn't hesitate one second, catching him with a picture-perfect left uppercut that whipped his head back like he'd slammed on the brakes in a speeding car. He dropped to his knees and she aimed a kick at his face that sent one of his teeth flying. He curled up on the floor in a fetal position, holding his bleeding face.

Miranda took a step back, raising her fists in a fighting stance, daring anyone to hit her back. She was a girl and everyone knew you didn't hit girls. Everyone except *The Unrest.* Mack began crossing the dancefloor, moving in to protect her, though he knew she wasn't the type of girl who usually needed protection. It was just his instinct.

A large skinhead with a big scraggly black beard stepped forward and punched Miranda in the jaw. She dropped like she'd been zapped with a taser. Several of the skinheads began to stomp and kick her. Mack couldn't believe it.

"You fucking cowards! You beat up a fucking girl!"

He hurled himself at the big Nazi fuck who'd punched Miranda in the jaw, kicking him in the chest and knocking him backwards into his buddies. He caught his balance and came back at Mack, swinging with both fists. Mack ducked the first two punches but was caught by the third. The blow felt like it could have taken his head off. The guy hit like a fucking mule.

I can't take too many more punches like that. I've got to end this shit quick, Mack thought. Besides the potential damage to himself a long fight might have caused, there was also the fact that Miranda was still down and the other skinheads were still beating on her. Mack ended the fight in the most expedient manner he could think of. He kicked the big skinhead in the knee with a sidekick, driving through the patella and snapping tendons with a satisfying "Pop!" that dropped the big Nazi bastard onto his ass, howling in pain.

Other punks that Mack knew from the scene came rushing into the pit to meet the skinheads. Norm, a guy from Mack's neighborhood who dressed almost like a skinhead himself, in a bomber jacket and black combat boots but with dreadlocks forming small bangs at the front of his otherwise shaved head, charged into the pit. Bilal Muhammed, a big black guy Mack knew from high school, who was almost as tall as Mack though considerably softer, leapt in, combat boots

10

first, immediately knocking three skinheads to the ground who got up throwing punches. A small white kid with short black hair with white polka dots named Clayton Dillard that also went to Mack's high school leapt into the fray, followed by damn near every punk in the place. It looked like a scene from *Westside Story* only without the dancing and a lot less Puerto Ricans.

Mack rushed at the surging horde of skinheads, aiming straight for Miranda. She was still down and still being pummeled. There was blood leaking from her nose, mouth, and ears. It didn't look good.

"Miranda!" Mack yelled as he fought his way to her. His fists collided with flesh and one body after another collapsed onto the dance floor to be trampled by the crowd. Mack took several punches and kicks on his way through the crowd of skinheads. His nose and lip were bleeding and his jaw throbbed in pain. Every time he took a few steps toward her, he was knocked back as he was attacked by someone else. He took a combat boot to the stomach that dropped him to his knees where he received another boot to the side of the head that turned everything dark for a moment. Mack didn't know who hit him but he quickly clamored back to his feet and struck the nearest skinhead. He grabbed the guy by the front of his jacket and punched him in the face repeatedly, fist pistoning up and down, reducing the guy's face to bloody hamburger until finally the skinhead stopped moving. Mack looked at the guy before he let go of him and allowed him to fall to the floor. Both the skinhead's eyes had swollen shut and his mouth was a bloody ruin. One of the guy's teeth had punctured through his lip, driven through by Mack's fist. A couple of his other teeth were lodged in Mack's knuckle. Mack plucked them out of his skin as he looked around to regain his bearings. He'd lost sight of Miranda and could no longer find her. Mack took another punch to the back of the head that caused him to stagger forward.

That's what I get for stopping to admire my work.

There was a large group of skinheads with their backs to him and Mack leapt into the air, landing with his knees on the shoulders of a large skin who looked like a linebacker, shorter than Mack but twice as wide. The guy fell forward and landed face first with Mack still on his back. The skinhead's face smashed into the dance floor, spraying blood in a huge star pattern. Mack turned to face the next one and the next, punching and kicking wildly.

"Miranda!" Mack yelled. He still couldn't see her anywhere. The crowd was now a full-scale riot. Someone turned on the house lights. The band stopped playing as chairs began to fly and someone toppled one of the large speakers on the side of the stage. The bouncers joined the fray, attacking skinheads and punks alike. A guy named Chris that Mack knew from the comic book store on South Street, rushed up to him and stood back to back with Mack, swinging at anyone and anything.

"What are you doing?"

"I'm covering your back. You just saved my ass back there. Thanks. Those Nazi fucks were about to kill me before you jumped in and started whoopin' ass. They had me surrounded. I owe you, man. Really. Thanks."

Mack didn't know that they had been about to beat the shit out of Chris when he'd jumped in. He didn't particularly like Chris and certainly wouldn't have risked his life for the guy. He had thought that Miranda was in the middle of that circle of skinheads, not this douchebag.

Fuck it. Let him think what he wants.

The sounds of battle echoed all around him as punks and skinheads went to war. Mack felt like a warrior, like a fucking Zulu on an ancient battlefield. He lived for this shit.

"Mack! Mack!" Jason ran up to him and grabbed him by the shoulders. His eyes were wide. He looked like he'd seen a ghost.

"What's up, Demon? Did you find Miranda? She went down and those fucking skinhead bastards were stomping her. Did you see her?"

"Your shirt! You're bleeding!"

The skintight black muscle-shirt that Mack was wearing had been sliced down the center and there was blood all over his torso from his neck to his waist. It looked like he'd been stabbed. Mack ran his palm down his chest, wiping away the blood. There was no wound.

"It ain't my blood."

Jason laughed.

"Did you see Miranda?"

"No, man. I didn't see her."

"Go look for her, man! We've got to help her!"

Mack turned toward the pit and charged back into battle. A few seconds later, he finally made it to Miranda. The skinheads were retreating leaving her crumpled on the dancefloor, her face had been pounded into a bruised, bleeding mess. Blood dripped steadily from her mouth and nose and she lay on her side with her eyes closed, unmoving. Mack scooped her up in his arms and ran for the front door.

"Call an ambulance! Someone call a fucking ambulance!"

She was barely breathing. Mack felt like his heart was breaking. Tears streamed down his face. Jason, Chris, Norm, Breezy, Alexis, Bilal, and a dozen other punks stared at him as he raced through the club with Miranda's limp body in his arms. None of them had ever seen Mack cry before. Mack could not remember the last time he had. There was no doubt in his mind now that he was in love with Miranda. He only hoped that she would live.

ONE

South Street, 12: 07 am, two weeks later

It was midnight on South Street. Locals, tourists, suburbanites, thugs of every race, would-be-mafioso, hippies, goths, punks, and skinheads crowded the snow-covered streets. Storefront windows featuring leather-clad manikins in leashes and handcuffs, trench coats and miniskirts, sporting chainsaws and machetes, were mixed with the normal ice cream and Italian water-ice shops and landmark cheese steak hoagie restaurants. The sidewalks were packed with people, shopping, eating, partying, trying to hook up or just hanging out. It looked more like a crowded nightclub than a city street.

The police had begun closing the street to vehicles after ten pm on weekends. There were so many people that cars would have been unable to get through even if the streets had been open. Police patrolled the crowds, though they seemed to spend more time lounging in the many pizza joints and bars that lined the streets then walking the sidewalks. When they were patrolling, they looked scared. On South Street, riots were known to erupt with little provocation. And the Philly PD were frequent casualties.

South Street, running from Eighth Street to Front Street, was the nearest commercial district to the waterfront. Up until the nineteen seventies brought the city's big push for urban renewal, it was a questionable, counter-culture, community populated by an eclectic mix of artists, musicians, criminals, derelicts, prostitutes, tricks and sailors (who were often one and the same) and the tourists who came to the riverfront to

14

listen to live music, shop the odd little shops that sprang up on the street, get drunk at the many bars, and gawk at the freaks and rift-raft. That part hadn't changed much. Then, the stores on South Street were mostly sole proprietorships, quirky knick-knack shops, antique stores, a plethora of bars, bizarre clothing stores, and adult boutiques that catered mostly to strippers, rebellious teenagers, and housewives looking to put a little spice back in the bedroom. In the 1980s, punk rock stores like *Skinz* and *Zipperheads* sprang up to replace many of the artsy boutiques, though most of the bars remained and a few new stores like *Unique Clothing, Blacks,* and *Trash & Vaudeville* sprang up to replace the ones that left. But slowly, retail chain stores like *Tower Records* and *Foot Locker,* which catered primarily to the tourists who flocked to South Street for the notorious nightlife, began to move in and the "neighborhood" community aspect of South Street began to disintegrate.

The trendier the street became, the angrier Mack and Jason grew. South Street was their home. It wasn't just part of the hardcore scene in Philly. It *was* the hardcore scene. And now it was slowly being taken over by jocks, tourists, poseurs and fucking skinheads.

"You're a big, black, faggot!" the kid with the shaved head said, pointing at the large silver hoop earrings in Mack's left ear. He was taller than Mack, but as thin as a junkie, with a weak chin, stooped shoulders and a bowed chest. His eyes swam in his head, unable to fix on anything. He was clearly drunk off his ass.

"Oh shit," Jason said, cupping a hand over his mouth. He looked as surprised as Mack was. He stared at the kid as if he had lost his mind. When he looked up at Mack, whose mouth had dropped open wide in disbelief before slowly contorting into a snarl, Jason almost appeared afraid. Mack knew better though, Jason loved to see him pulverize assholes, the more brutal the better. He was more than an enabler. Jason was usually the instigator. He treated Mack like an attack dog that he sicced on anyone who threatened or offended him. Mack didn't mind though. Fighting was one of his few talents and like all talents, if you didn't use it, you lost it.

"What did you just say to me?"

Someone was about to catch a bad one.

Mack looked at the kid. He didn't look much like a skinhead. He wore a leather motorcycle jacket and motorcycle boots instead of a bomber jacket and Doc Martins. He looked more like a punk rocker with a shaved head than a white supremacist, definitely not a member of *The Unrest,* but there was the little matter of the insult. If he wasn't a Nazi skinhead, he sure as shit talked like one.

"I said, you're a big, black, faggot!"

They were standing outside South Philly Deli. It was a Philadelphia landmark. The big window with the image of the Liberty Bell wrapped in the American flag, had been seen on South Street for more than twenty years. It was one of the restaurants you had to visit when you came to South Street along with Pat's Steaks and Genarro's Pizza. The restaurant was packed with tourists stuffing their mouths with Italian hoagies, roast beef sandwiches, Ruben's, and turkey hoagies. They all screamed and leapt from their seats when the skinhead's face smashed through the window, shattering it into a thousand jagged shards, many of which lodged in the guy's face. He collapsed onto the sidewalk, yelling and picking glass from his bloody forehead, cheeks, and lips. His face looked like it had been put through a meat grinder. Large gashes gushed blood and tiny strips of flesh were peeled back revealing the pink flesh beneath.

Mack ducked into the crowd, wiping his bloody fists on his jeans as he raced down the street with Jason close behind, howling and laughing.

"Oh my, God! That was AWESOME! You fucked 'em up bad, dude!"

Mack was quiet, his head swiveled back and forth, shoulders hunched, eyes searching the street, hoping he could get off South Street before the cops arrived. The police in South Philly weren't terribly tenacious. Between the Italian Mafia, the Irish Mob and the Junior Black Mafia, most of them were on the take and on South Street, making an arrest was always dangerous. The cops tried to avoid it at all costs. Unless it was something like murder, if they didn't catch you in the act or in the first two or three hours following the crime, you were home free. But if they did catch you, a serious beating was not unheard of. They wouldn't give a damn about what he'd done to the skinhead, but vandalizing the South Philly Deli window could very well get him a police baton enema.

They turned the corner onto Third Street. When he looked back, Mack was not surprised to see that no one was chasing them. Once you were off the main street, the neighborhood looked very much as it had thirty years ago, dark and dangerous. After sunset, most people avoided the side streets.

"Let's go further up South Street where it's not so crowded. We can hang out at the comic store. Chris is working until midnight."

"It is midnight."

Jason shrugged.

"He's probably still there. Dude loves comics. If he didn't work there he'd still be hanging out there all day."

Mack nodded.

"Yeah, okay, but then we need to go back to Third and South. Those chicks from Jersey are still up there and Breezy and Alexis get off work soon."

"You've got a thing for Alexis don't you?" Jason asked.

"She's fine, man. But she never looks twice at me. Fuck her."

"Yeah, fuck that bitch!" He smiled. "The very first chance

17

you get. Fuck her real hard,"

Mack laughed.

"You're a fool, man."

A silence fell between them.

"You been to see Miranda lately?"

Mack nodded solemnly.

"Yeah. She's still in a coma but they say her CAT scans look normal. It doesn't look like there's any brain damage. She could come out of it any day."

"That's good. That's real good."

Jason was staring at Mack as they walked down the dark street on their way to the comic shop. Steam billowed from the sewers, giving the streets a London fog effect that made Mack think of vampires and Jack the Ripper.

"You're in love with Miranda ain't you?"

Mack nodded.

"Yeah. I think I am."

"Why didn't you ever tell her?"

"Cause I'm black and she's white and not everyone's cool with that. I'm not even that mildly acceptable light-skinned color like Prince or Michael Jackson. I'm fucking black, black."

"Man, Miranda's not like that. She's not prejudice or nothin'."

"I know that. I ain't sayin' she is. Look, people won't say it, especially not to my face, but I know a lot of white chicks, even if they ain't prejudice, just don't find black guys attractive, especially not dark-skinned black guys like me. I just didn't want to hear her say some shit about wanting to be just friends or to find out she really had a crush on you or something. That shit would have fucked me up."

Jason continued staring at Mack. So long that it became uncomfortable.

"What, man? Why you staring at me like that?"

"I didn't know your big ass was so sensitive. When she

wakes up, you gotta tell her."

"Maybe."

"No, maybe. Tell her!"

"I don't know. I don't do rejection well."

"Just tell her, dude. You'll hate yourself if you don't."

Mack snickered.

"I've been hating myself for years."

TWO

The Broad Street subway station, 4:13 AM

Bo, Skinner, and Little Davey followed the old black woman across the subway platform. Graffiti marred every visible surface and the smell of urine was almost overpowering. The metal on steel shriek of subway trains traveling distant rails echoed through the station. Foul smelling winds whipped out of the tunnels. Little Davey giggled to himself, laughing at some private joke that only he was privy to, thinking up something gruesome to do to the old woman. Bo and Skinner shared a worried look. It was never good when Davey was in this kind of mood. He had a tendency to take things too far.

The three of them were dressed identically in white t-shirts, green bomber jackets, black Levis cuffed at the bottom, and oxblood Doc Martin combat boots. Little Davey completed the look with red suspenders, a thick leather belt with a chrome swastika belt buckle, and a black bowler hat. If their group could be said to have a leader, it was Little Davey. He wasn't the biggest or the strongest of them, but he was by far the most ruthless and that commanded Bo and Skinner's respect. Either one of them could have kicked Little Davey's ass but he was likely to retaliate by slitting their throats, cutting off their cocks and shoving it into the wound.

All three had shaved heads. They went to great pains to follow the skinhead aesthetic down to the last detail. Little Davey was clean-shaven while Skinner wore a goatee and Big Bo had a scraggly red beard that made him look like a lumberjack. They were members of a skinhead group from

20

Camden, New Jersey called *The Unrest* and tonight, they were out to start a war.

"Hurry up! You want this old bitch to get away?" Little Davey asked.

"Naw. I'm coming." Bo answered.

The threesome stumbled across the subway platform. They had been drinking all night and had left Skinner's apartment looking for something to vent their aggression on, which was bad news for anything weak and helpless they happened to stumble upon, like the withered septuagenarian in the ratty gray wool coat, thick black orthopedic shoes and flower print headscarf, all by herself in the middle of the subway platform. It was four o'clock in the morning and she was alone. It was just her and them. The moment they spotted her, they knew they were going to hurt her.

Bo drained the rest of his beer. Budweiser. A good American Beer. He crushed the can and tossed it onto the subway tracks. The clang of the aluminum can hitting the steel rails echoed, sounding even louder in the stillness of the night. They were almost out of alcohol. They'd spent most of the evening drinking Jack Daniels and Wild Turkey that Skinner's dad had leftover from his New Year's Eve party. They were past buzzed and well into the land of drunk and disorderly. "Feeling ten-feet tall and bulletproof" as Little Davey liked to say. Their courage as well as their rage amplified tenfold by whiskey and beer.

"She's probably on her way to a job that Affirmative Action helped her to get over a better qualified white person," Davey thought, already searching his mind for the proper rationale for the coming violence. He giggled again as he imagined increasingly brutal ways to impress his friends and sate his own need for terror and destruction.

Beside him, Bo still held the bottle of Wild Turkey clutched by the neck as they walked across the subway platform. The big bearded skinhead took several more swigs of the amber liquid and grimaced in pain as it scalded his throat. Davey knew what the big guy was doing. He was drowning his mind in booze in preparation for the violence he knew was about to go down. Bo was the type of guy who needed alcohol to dull his normal human tendency toward sympathy and compassion. Little Davey didn't need any such chemical assistance. He had no sympathy or compassion to hinder him.

"Ease up on the booze. If you pass out we're leaving you here. You're too damn big to carry," Davey said.

Bo was about 6'3" and every bit of 250lbs. He loved football and had played on teams in elementary school and junior high but had been afraid to go out for the team in high school. It was one of the many things he blamed the black kids at his school for. They had terrorized him into giving up his dream of winning a college scholarship and then playing for Notre Dame or the Texas Longhorns before his ultimate dream of playing for the NFL. Now he was just another dumb redneck with no future, all because he had let those coons intimidate him. Little Davey felt sorry for him. His resentment about his aborted football career had been the thing that Davey used to talk him into joining *The Unrest.* Skinner had been easier. He was just tired of getting his ass kicked and Davey promised that they would protect him.

All night they'd been talking about the impending race war. It was inevitable, Little Davey concluded. There was no way to avoid it. And it was all because of desegregation. If it wasn't for desegregation they would not have all wound up at a predominantly black high school getting teased, bullied, and beaten every day. Instead, high school had been hell. And now that they were out of school, it was time for some pay back.

The old lady, was to be the first casualty of their war against the black race. She was the enemy, part of the race that was stealing jobs from the white man, that was breeding with whites and polluting their pure Aryan blood with their inferior DNA, that was destroying America with their drugs and gangs and criminal behavior. She was part of the race that had taken Bo's lunch every day. Part of the race that had stolen Skinner's sneakers right off his feet and sent him home in bare socks when he'd come to school in a new pair of Air Jordans. The old woman was part of the race that had put Little Davey in the hospital for using the "N-word" when a big black kid named Harold had tried to steal his silver necklace, the one his mother had given him for Christmas. They had to be destroyed for America to survive and return to her former glory and that meant there must be a war, a cleansing by fire. America had to be purged of all the "mud people", the niggers, spics, Jews, and Arabs and all the atheists and homosexuals.

"Here, little monkey. Come here, little monkey." Little Davey tittered.

The old lady walked faster, casting worried glances over her shoulder at the group of leering teenaged delinquents. She clutched her pocketbook tight to her chest as she sped up, hurrying down toward the end of the platform, praying to God the train would come before she ran out of places to go. Unfortunately, God didn't hear her. The three skinheads grinned at her as she came to the end of the platform.

"Where you going, little monkey? Don't you want to play?"

"You boys stay away from me. I don't want no trouble."

"Oh but we do, you dirty little ape. We want trouble." Little Davey said as he drew closer to her.

"I'll call the police!"

"And how will you do that?" Bo asked. "Ain't no phones down here."

"No. It looks to me like it's just you and us. But I'll tell you what, since all you nigger bitches are a bunch of whores anyway. You suck us all off and we won't hurt you. We'll let you go," Little Davey said.

"Awww. That's nasty! I ain't lettin' this wrinkled up old coon suck my dick. She looks like she's a hundred years old!" Skinner said with an expression of revulsion twisting his face. At 17 Skinner was the youngest. He still had another year in high school. He was always the one who tried to chicken out whenever they had anything dangerous or criminal planned though Little Davey knew that Skinner was a sadist. Skinner had confessed to him that he liked to torture cats and had even cut the balls off a stray dog once. Skinner wasn't afraid of violence. He loved it. It was jail that Skinner was afraid of. He was short, almost as short as Little Davey, and he was skinny and wore glasses.

"If I ever go to jail I'll get raped. Look at me!" Skinner said once when they were talking about kidnapping and killing black kids like The Atlanta Child Murderer.

"That guy had balls. He had the right idea," Skinner said, "But there's no way I could do that."

"If you went to prison you'd just hook up with the Aryan Brotherhood. They'd protect you." Little Davey answered, trying to reassure him. The idea of kidnapping and torturing black kids had its appeal and he didn't want to rule it out. Though he wasn't sure how they'd ever get away with something like that. A man could dream though.

"Yeah, and then you'd be their bitch. At least then you'd be sucking on a white cock instead of a big black one," Bo said and laughed.

Little Davey smiled. He wasn't letting Skinner chicken out this time.

"Every woman is beautiful with my dick in her mouth. You just imagine it's somebody else, like Madonna or that chick from *Married With Children*. It'll be just like jackin' off, only with this old nigger's mouth instead of your hand."

Bo and Skinner both looked horrified but then they began to warm to the idea. Davey could see it in their eyes

24

and the stupid grins on their faces. He knew Skinner was a virgin and as ugly as this old bitch was, he would have let her wrap her big black monkey lips around his little pecker in an instant. Little Davey looked around the subway station. It was still empty. He unzipped his pants, pulled his cock out and waved it at the old lady. She looked at it in horror as if he had pulled a gun out of his pants.

"Come on, nigger. Get down here and suck it. Don't try and tell me you don't know how. I bet you sucked more cocks than you can remember as old as you are."

Despite himself, Little Davey was starting to get aroused. Then the old lady spit at him.

"You disgusting heathen! You should be ashamed of yourselves. I'm calling the cops. Heeeellllp! Helllllp!"

Little Davey tucked his penis back into his pants, more than a little disappointed that she hadn't gone for it. Since his girlfriend left him a year ago, he'd only had his dick sucked once by an older girl who lived down the street and it had been incredible. As old and wrinkled as this old lady was, he was sure he would have cum just the same if she had wrapped her lips around his cock. He had been fantasizing about shoving it down her throat and choking her with it.

"Oh, well. It looks like we're going to have to hurt you then."

Little Davey snatched the bottle of Wild Turkey from Bo and poured it on the old woman's head. He watched impassively as she cursed and sputtered, drowning in alcohol. Then he threw the bottle out onto the train track. The old woman winced when the glass shattered. Little Davey reached into his pocket for his Zippo lighter then set her hair ablaze. The flame quickly engulfed her face and then her coat. Her screams filled the train station.

"Oh shit!" Bo yelled.

"What the fuck, man! What did you do that for?" Skinner whined.

Little Davey was silent. He stared in amazement as the old woman's face began to melt and her eyeballs sizzled and popped like eggs in a microwave. The war had begun.

THREE

The squat house, 3:35 AM

The wind sounded sad and angry, violent, like a tortured spirit raging against existence. Mack could hear the thunder of drums and the wail of guitars in the wind's howl. He could almost put lyrics to it, something fast, rebellious, defiant like speed metal or hardcore. It was the kind of night where lovers huddled up beneath blankets in front of a roaring fireplace and kids sipped cocoa and fantasized about Christmas. It was the kind of night that chased the homeless into shelters or froze them to the sidewalk. The kind of night that brought all the punks in from South Street to escape the cold.

Mack sat on the couch with a 40 ounce bottle of Colt .45 on his lap, tracing the twin daggers crossed through his belt buckle with his free hand and daydreaming about Miranda. The last time he'd been to the hospital to see her, he held her hand and wept for twenty minutes. Mack was still crying when he walked out of the hospital. He felt like he should have saved her, like he should have gotten to her sooner. Mack wondered if he spent too much time kicking the shit out of those skinheads, started to like it too much, and forgot about her for just a second, carried away by his lust for violence. Maybe if he threw a few less punches, he would have gotten to her sooner. He replayed it over and over again in his head, editing it down to see where time could've been cut out, where he over-indulged himself in the violence at the expense of Miranda. Mack didn't know what he would do if she didn't get better. He took another long swig from the bottle then put it back in his lap. It was the only bottle of

Colt left and he was protecting it. He walked all the way up to South Street to get it. Malt liquor was a rare commodity in this neighborhood.

The Dead Milkmen sang about their *"Bitchin' Camaro"* as Jason danced around the living room, kicking and stomping in his black Doc Martins, trying to start up a mosh pit right there in the middle of the house. Mack laughed and raised his forty in salute.

"Slam, baby! Slam!" he yelled.

"Yeeeaaah!"

Jason howled and jumped into the air with both feet, coming down with a huge bang that echoed through the empty walls. Jason was more than a best friend to Mack, that crazy white boy was just like family. He was the one who'd gotten Mack into the punk rock scene. Before the two of them became friends, Mack had been lost and alone, pissed off at the world and headed for trouble as sure as if he was a bullet that had been aimed and fired. They ran into each other on South Street the previous summer when Jason was begging for beer money. It was almost midnight and Mack was wandering South Street by himself, trying to pick up girls without much luck, when he heard Jason call to him.

Mack had seen the kid around school but had never spoken a word to him. They were from different worlds, worlds that seldom crossed. Mack was born in Germantown, G-Town a black ghetto on the northwest side of town. Jason was from South Philly. He grew up with Italians on one side, the Irish on the other, and Jews in between. It was a working class neighborhood but far from a ghetto. Through four years of high school, they had both assumed that they had nothing in common. This was the first time Jason had ever spoken to him.

"Hey, Mack! You got a couple bucks, man? We need some beer!"

Jason was amongst a small group of punks, anarchists,

mostly atheists, anti-everything except music, alcohol, sex, and drugs, sitting on the sidewalk outside the drugstore on 5th and South streets. He laughed after he said it, obviously expecting the big black kid to tell him to fuck off. Mack surprised him when he walked over to him and pulled out two hundred dollars.

"How much you want?"

"Oh, shit."

That night, Mack spent his entire paycheck on beer and the anemic-looking teenager in leather and spikes showed him all kinds of interesting ways to vent his frustration at the world. The best of which, was beating up skinheads. Now, the two were inseparable.

Jason was the exact opposite of Mack who looked like he belonged on a basketball court instead of amongst a group of punk rockers. Jason was short, skinny, and pale, with long limp black hair that hung down into his face and a mouthful of metal braces. He had wounded puppy-dog eyes that made women want to nurture and protect him and made men uncomfortable. There were storms in his eyes as Breezy often said. Mack would never admit it, but those sad eyes were the entire reason they were friends. Every time Mack looked at Jason he wanted to hug him, which he hoped didn't make him gay. He and Jason joked that if they ever became gay they would fuck each other first. It hadn't happened yet. The closest they'd ever come to anything gay was fucking the same girl, but they hadn't even touched. They had stared into each other's eyes, smiling nervously as they used the girl like a pair of Chinese finger cuffs.

Two guys that Mack didn't know were dancing around with Jason, friends of his from South Street. One of them had a shaved head and wore a bomber jacket and black Doc Martins. His name was Billy and he said he wasn't a racist skinhead even though he looked like one. He was a SHARP (Skinheads Against Racial Prejudice) skin. Mack didn't trust him though.

Why dress like a piece of shit if you weren't a piece of shit?

The other guy had bright green hair that stood up in huge spikes. He spoke with a British accent that Mack suspected was fake but the girls fell for it. They were swooning over him most of the night and listening to his stories about "The real punk scene" in London.

"My mates in South London had a band that once opened for *The Sex Pistols*. I used to see Johnny Rotten at parties all the time. He and I have the same birthday, ya know? January thirty-first."

"Will you shut the fuck up? Don't you get tired of hearing yourself talk? Damn." Chris yelled.

"I like hearing him talk. I love his accent," said a girl they'd picked up on South Street. Mack had seen her at a few shows but didn't know her name. She was dressed in a plaid miniskirt with white leggings and a white turtleneck sweater. She looked like she'd been standing in the middle of a GAP when it exploded. In contrast, her jet black hair had streaks of purple and pink in it and she had about a dozen earrings in each ear and big silver rings on each finger, including a ring with an eyeball in it that reminded Mack of something from the Tolkien Trilogy.

"Then fuck him or something. Maybe that will keep his ass quiet." Mack said.

"Okay!" she replied, grinning. She took the British guy's hand and led him upstairs.

"Damn. Why don't I have it like that?"

"Because all the bitches are scared that your dick is as big as your biceps," Jason said, laughing.

"It's bigger than yours, Demon."

Demon was Mack's nickname for Jason. Ever since he'd started calling him that the name had stuck and now everyone called him Demon.

"How do you know? You peekin' in my drawers when I'm asleep?"

"I already told you. If I ever turn gay, I ain't gonna ask. I'm just gonna take. And your sweet white ass is first."

Jason bent over.

"Come and get it."

Without budging from the couch, Mack stretched out his leg and kicked Jason in the ass.

"Begone, Demon!"

"Damn, homes! Why you gotta do me like that? You know you want this."

Mack laughed harder. He always thought it was funny when Jason tried to talk like he was black. It got on his nerves sometimes, especially when he started quoting Public Enemy lyrics. But that was just how Jason was. Mack knew the kid idolized him. As soon as they became friends Jason had immersed himself in all things African American, including hip-hop and malt liquor. He even smoked *Kools.* Mack had reciprocated somewhat by embracing the punk rock scene. He'd become a fan of *Black Flag, Skinny Puppy, The Dead Kennedys, The Sex Pistols, Ministry* and Philadelphia's own *Dead Milkmen.* Now, he seldom listened to hip-hop unless Jason was playing it.

The music changed from *The Dead Milkmen* to a group called *The Screaming Trees.* Jason and the skinhead were now the only ones dancing. Mack kept a close eye on the guy. There was something about him besides his shaved head that bothered Mack. He'd seen the guy snorting PCP earlier. That shit made people crazy.

The living room was packed with people. Most of them were friends of Jason's but many were new faces they'd picked up throughout the night. There were three girls from Cherry Hill sitting on the floor, tripping on acid, who had been there for a couple days. Jason was high too. He'd had a couple tabs of LSD earlier in the evening. Acid was Jason's favorite high. He only dropped acid when Mack was around though. He knew Mack would protect him if he had a bad trip.

31

Mack was the only one in the party who wasn't trippin' on something. Alcohol was the only thing he would touch and he was even starting to wonder if he drank too much. His biggest fear was losing control. Winding up some drunken homeless derelict had always been the thing that scared him the most. He took another swig from the bottle of Colt .45 then screwed the cap back on it and hugged it to his chest.

They had been squatting in the old house for two weeks. It had been snowing off and on the entire time so Jason and Mack had spent most of the last two weeks indoors except for the occasional appearance on South Street. They were starting to go stir crazy. Mack had an outlet because he could still go home whenever he wanted to. He hadn't run away from home or been kicked out like most of the other kids. They had no home to go to. This house was their only home.

At any given moment there were upwards of a dozen people squatting in the house with them. All punk kids from the scene. Some of them were suburban kids from the main line. Some of them were kids who'd come over the bridge from New Jersey and stayed. The only thing any of them had in common was a love for hardcore music and a hatred for authority. But that was enough.

The house belonged to a friend named Rachael. Or it had. Her name was still on the lease but she hadn't been there in weeks and nobody had paid the rent. She had thrown a party a few weeks ago and they'd all come, partied like rock stars, and never left. None of them had seen Rachael or any of her roommates since. As odd as it seemed, they had all moved in and the people who actually rented the house had moved out. Now it was their house until someone told them different.

They were all part of a dying breed of punk rockers. The 1980s were coming to a close and punk rock was dying a slow death. Heavy Metal and Hip-hop had taken over as the new sound of youthful rebellion. Jason, Mack and the rest of their friends were doing their best to keep the scene alive. They were all getting older though. South Street was slowly becoming one long strip-mall. Skinheads, guidos, thugs, and suburbanites were taking over the place. But Jason and Mack weren't giving it up without a fight. In Philly, South Street and punk rock were nearly synonymous and they were convinced that one could not survive without the other.

A friend of theirs named Chris, who was the only Puerto Rican punk rocker Mack had ever heard of, stood with two other girls from the scene, huddled in a corner, whispering. All three of them had Mohawks. Breezy, a 16-year-old runaway who worked at the burger joint on South Street, had a huge platinum Mohawk. Alexis, a chubby girl with huge tits who hung out with them on the weekends then went back to her exclusive private school in Chestnut Hill during the week, had her hair up in a wicked-looking jet black Mohawk with bleached blond tips. Chris had a Mohawk consisting of five huge blonde spikes that he styled with crazy glue and "Dippity-Do". Mack took another swig of Colt .45 then leered at Alexis's tits.

"Damn, girl. Your tits are fuckin' crazy! I'd suck the skin off those motherfuckers!" Mack joked.

Chris looked like he swallowed his own tongue.

"Man, why are you so nasty?"

"Why are you such a pussy?"

"You need to show women more respect."

"No, I need to show them this!"

Mack leaned back on the couch, unzipped his pants and pulled his cock out. He stroked it a little and waggled it at the girls.

"Ewwww!" the girls sang in chorus.

Mack laughed.

"Cut that shit out, man. You're fucking sick!" Chris yelled.

"Oh, shit! You're crazy, dude!" Jason laughed, pointing

at Mack's limp dick lolling from his open fly. The Jersey girls who were sitting on the floor just stared at him. One of them leaned over and rubbed the head of his cock until it stiffened.

"Your dick is beautiful." She sighed. Her eyes were glossy and there was a faraway expression in them.

Mack laughed again

"Thanks. Your mouth is beautiful. Maybe we should introduce them to each other?"

She giggled.

"You're too funny."

"Yeah, I'm funny. But I really would like a blowjob."

She giggled again and wagged a finger at him. Everyone laughed, except Chris who shook his head in disgust.

"Man, put that shit away!"

"I'm just fuckin' around. Stop actin' like a little bitch. The girls don't mind. Do you?"

Breezy and Alexis shook their heads and laughed. The three girls on the floor had already gone back to watching the trails their fingers left in the air.

"That's just how Mack is. He's crazy as fuck, but that's why we love him. He didn't mean anything by it. Besides, everybody knows he's in love with Miranda," Breezy said.

"Is that why, Alexis won't fuck me?" Mack said, looking directly at Alexis who was staring at Chris, clearly enamored with the handsome Puerto Rican. She heard her name and finally turned her head.

"What?"

"Nothing."

"He said he wants to fuck you." Breezy said.

"It's true. I do."

"You're sick." Chris said, still scowling.

"Everybody just chill. Everything's cool."

"Yeah, Chris. Stop trippin'. I kind of like you. I'd hate to have to kick your ass," Mack said, laughing.

"Who's Miranda?" one of the Jersey girls asked.

"None of your fuckin' business," Mack replied.

From the other side of the room there was a loud banging noise. It sounded like a body had fallen.

"What the fuck is wrong with you!" Jason yelled.

Mack jumped up from the couch, tucking his penis back into his jeans. He pushed Chris and Alexis aside so he could see what Jason was yelling about. The skinhead was going berserk, banging his head against the walls and smearing them with blood.

"What the fuck is wrong with this idiot?" Jason asked.

"He was snortin' dust earlier. He's wacked out."

"Help me get him outside, Mack."

"It's like two degrees out there."

"I don't give a fuck. He's about to fuck up the whole crib!"

"Shit. I don't give a fuck either. You want him out. He's out."

Mack walked over to the skinhead, grabbed him by the back of his pants and the back of his shirt and lifted him off the ground.

"Demon! Open the front door!"

Jason hurried to the door and opened it. It was snowing outside and there were already two or three inches on the ground.

"You can't throw him out there! He'll freeze to death!" Alexis shouted.

Mack ignored her and tossed the skinhead out the door and onto the sidewalk. Billy landed on a pile of trash, knocking it over and spilling out into the street. Mack shut the door.

"That stupid-ass motherfucker."

He and Jason bumped fists and laughed.

"Fuck 'em. I hope he does freeze."

Mack resumed his position on the couch. The Colt .45 was half gone.

"Did one of you motherfuckers drink my forty?"

"You drank it, fool!" Chris answered.

Something hit the front door and shattered. Everyone jumped.

"Shit! What was that?"

Jason ran to the door and looked out the window.

"That's fucking Billy. His ass is going crazy out there, throwing bottles and shit. Somebody's gonna call the cops. I've got warrants. We gotta let him back in."

"Shit! I'm sick of this fool!"

Mack and Jason got up and opened the door.

"Get your stupid ass in here!" Jason shouted.

"No! I know you don't want me around. Nobody wants me around!"

He picked up another bottle and threw it at the house.

"Then go the fuck home!"

"I don't have a fucking home!"

"Look," Mack interrupted, "Either get your ass inside or move along. You can't be out here making all this noise and shit. And if you throw one more fucking bottle I'm gonna knock your dumb ass out and leave you in the snow to die. You hear me? Think I'm playin'!"

"Fuck you, Mack! You can't do nothin' to me. I ain't scared of you."

The skinhead began shadow boxing in the snow then slipped and fell down onto his ass. He laid back in the snow and closed his eyes.

Mack stormed off the porch and grabbed Billy by the throat, jerking him up off the ground.

"Get your ass inside. Now!"

He dragged Billy into the house and shut the door.

"I don't want him in here fucking up shit," Jason said.

"Then what do you want to do with him?"

"Throw him in the basement."

Mack dragged Billy over to the basement door. Billy

tried to dig his heels in and hold onto the walls but Mack was too strong and muscled him out of the room and to the top of the basement stairs. Billy went limp, making Mack carry his dead weight.

"Walk, motherfucker!"

Mack punched him in the stomach, doubling Billy over and dropping him to his knees. Billy coughed and moaned and tried to curl into a fetal ball. Mack jerked him back up to his feet.

"Fuck this!" Jason said then gave Billy a shove that sent him tumbling down the stairs ass over ankles. He landed on the hard concrete floor with a loud "Thwap!" A small dark halo of blood formed around his head.

"Oh, shit. I think you killed him." Chills raced over his skin. His stomach twisted and the room tilted and spun. He felt like he was going to throw up. It wasn't the fact that he had just killed someone that made him feel faint and nauseous. He could care less about killing a skinhead. It was the fear of getting caught.

"Shhhh! Keep your fuckin' voice down. You want everybody in the house to know?" Jason whispered. He peeked around the corner into the living room, everyone was still getting high. Chris was trying to get laid and Breezy and the Jersey girls were on another planet.

Mack and Jason stood at the top of the stairs for almost a full minute, waiting for Billy to move. He didn't.

"His chest ain't movin'. Dude is dead." Mack whispered.

Jason shrugged. "Fuck it. Let's deal with it in the morning. We can dump him in the projects or something. The cops'll just think he got mugged."

Mack knew he made a lot of bad decisions since he started hanging out in the hardcore scene. He was working two jobs when he met Jason a year ago. He quit both of them a month later. Mack was supposed to have left for college in Ohio this past fall but he called the school and delayed his

37

admission by a year. Still, he knew that not calling the cops right then and there might just have been the worst mistake he ever made. If they hid Billy's body somewhere it would be an admission of guilt. They were about to turn a legitimate accident into a first degree homicide.

Demon is still high and drunk off his ass, but I'm not drunk yet. What's my excuse? Mack thought. Then he turned off the light in the basement and closed the door.

In for a penny. In for a pound.

FOUR

"Old-fuckin'-Milwaukee! That's all you can find in this damn neighborhood. Pabst Blue Ribbon and Old-fuckin'-Milwaukee. This shit tastes like piss! If I don't get some more Colt 45 soon I'm gonna kill a motherfucker!"

Mack hurled the empty forty-ounce bottle at the stone fireplace and smiled viciously, watching it shatter and spray shards of glass onto the carpet. Chris's huge platinum Mohawk was sticking out from beneath a blanket as he slept beside the fireplace in a drunken stupor. Tiny shards of glass rained down onto his head.

"Hey!"

"Shut the fuck up, Chris! Take your drunk ass back to sleep."

Chris rolled over, mumbling under his breath and pulling his leather jacket over his head to protect him from any further debris.

"Relax, dude. This is an Irish neighborhood. You ain't gonna find shit but whiskey and Old Milwaukee. That's just how that shit is here," Jason said. "Now you done scared the shit out of Chris. He probably pissed himself."

Mack snickered.

"Yeah. He probably did."

"We'll get some Colt 45 when we walk up to South Street later."

Mack smiled wide and nodded. Jason always knew how to mellow him out.

"Bet."

Mack was not a small kid. He was only eighteen years old but built like a middleweight boxer. Before he started hanging out with Jason and all his punk rock friends, he'd been working construction full time doing concrete and blacktop and working part-time at South Philadelphia Recreation Center, teaching weightlifting to young Italian kids, most of whom had parents in the Mafia. He'd been lifting weights since he was twelve years old when he bought his first weight set, one of those old vinyl sets filled with concrete, with the money he raised on his paper route. Since he joined the scene, the only time he went home was to eat, shower, and workout. The rest of the time, he stayed in shape by doing pushups with Jason sitting on his back. Jason only weighed about a hundred and twenty-five pounds. Mack could do twenty pushups easily with him on his back.

Back then, Mack's head was shaved on the sides with dreadlocks on top that he slathered in mousse so that they stuck straight up off his head. He wore black jeans, black motorcycle boots, a thick leather belt with two small daggers crossed through the belt buckle, no shirt and a leather motorcycle jacket he'd borrowed from Rachael, the girl who used to live at the house they were all squatting in. The jacket and the hair combined to give him the appearance of some sort of leather clad voodoo priest.

All the kids in the house looked to Mack for protection from the thugs, jocks, and, most importantly, the skinheads. Mack delighted in his role. It was the first time in his life that he'd ever felt like he fit in anywhere. Back in his own neighborhood, he felt like an outcast because he didn't use or sell drugs, didn't speak in one never ending stream of profanity-laced slang, and would rather read comic books and horror novels than watch The Sixers or The Eagles on TV. The only way he fit in was by fighting. Kicking the shit out of anyone who threatened his friends was his greatest joy in life.

Mack was the only black kid in the house and one of only five black punk rockers in the scene. That made him more than just an oddity. It made him fucking cool. Mack was the guy who could walk them all safely through the projects. He was the guy who could score them good weed from the kids in the Martin Luther King Projects at the other end of South Street. And whenever there was violence to be done, he was the one they all turned to. They felt safer having him in the house with them and he felt like he was part of something, a family, a culture, more so than he'd ever felt in the black community where he had always been an outcast.

"So, what are we gonna do about Billy?"

"Shhhhh! We have to wait until everybody leaves. Then we can sneak him out and hide him somewhere."

"How? We just gonna carry him through the street in broad-fucking-daylight? We ain't got no car."

"I'll see if I can borrow my dad's car."

"Oh yeah. Hi, Dad. It's me, your son that you haven't seen in six months. I just came back to borrow the car. You pull that shit off and you're the mutherfuckin' man."

"Doesn't Breezy have a car?"

"I don't know but I bet these Jersey bitches do."

"I don't even know their names."

"Didn't you fuck one of 'em last night?"

Jason shrugged.

"I still don't know her name."

"It doesn't matter. She had to get here somehow. I doubt she took a cab over the bridge. Ask her when she wakes up."

Jason smiled lopsidedly and looked at the floor, shuffling his feet bashfully.

"Ummm."

"What is it now?"

"I can't remember who she is."

"What?"

"I don't remember which one I fucked. I was drunk and I

was flirting with all three of 'em. I know I fucked one of 'em. I still smell like pussy and I remember putting a condom on. I remember I was fucking one of 'em doggy style and I couldn't come because I was so drunk. So she gave me head and I came down her throat. I just don't remember seeing her face."

"Am I the only one not getting fucked around here?" Mack yelled.

"Man, chill! We're trying to sleep!" Chris yelled back, pulling the blankets up higher.

"Even Chris got fucked last night. I hate this motherfucker. He fucked Alexis last night. Can you believe that? I wanted that bitch."

"It's racism!" Jason shouted.

"I'm starting to think it is, man." Mack was serious. For a moment, he looked like he was about to cry. He hadn't gotten any pussy in the two weeks they'd been squatting in the house, despite all the girls who'd come and gone. He'd made out with a few of them, but that was as far as it had gone. Mack rubbed his eyes and took a deep breath. He wasn't about to cry over pussy.

"I'm telling you, they're all afraid of the soul pole," Jason joked, hugging Mack and kissing him on the cheek.

"Yeah, whatever." He wasn't in the mood for jokes.

"I'm getting hungry," Jason said.

"There's no food."

"Let's just go up to South Street and pick up some more dumb suburban chicks and get them to buy us breakfast."

"Bet."

At that time, "dumb suburban chicks" who were desperate to rebel against their parents and hang out with real punk rockers, were their number one source of income. They bought them food, paid for their beer, and usually paid their way into punk rock shows at Club Revival, an old eighteenth century church downtown that had been converted into a punk rock club. When there were no girls around to pay for their beer and food, Jason would walk up to the train station at the Gallery Mall to panhandle. His puppy dog eyes made him a natural.

Jason was little and cute. He had the whole "Johnny Depp with an edge" thing going for him and when he wanted to, he could look downright pitiful. He would get thirty or forty bucks panhandling easily. Sometimes people even tried to take him home with them. He usually made enough in one hour to buy beer for the whole house. But it was too cold for that and the Jersey girls were broke. They'd paid for the beer and the drugs the last two nights but they had run out of money. It was time to replace them, but not before Jason and Mack used their car to transport a body.

Mack knew their lifestyle was unsustainable, but for now they were living the way they wanted to live: wild, free, with no one to answer to, no clocks to punch, and no schedule to keep. They slept when they were tired and woke up whenever they felt like it. It was the best time of their lives and it was all about to end.

"Let's just go up to South Street for a while and get some coffee at The Gathering Space. Padre should be there by now. Then we can see if there are any girls out. By then, the Jersey girls should be awake and we can borrow their car."

Mack put his arm around Jason and walked him into the dining room. He didn't want Chris to hear what he was about to say, just in case he was still awake. He would trip if he knew there was a corpse in the basement.

"Should we check on him? Cover him up or something? What if he starts to smell?"

"It's freezing down there. He ain't gonna rot. Not for a few days anyway. Let's just go and get back before everyone wakes up. I'm fuckin' starving!"

"Man. You're a trip. You're going to go stuff your face and then help me carry a body? What if we have to cut him up or something?"

Jason shrugged.

"Gotta do what we gotta do. I still need to eat."

South Street was dead. It was too early and no one was out yet except a smattering of school kids hanging out. Jason and Mack walked down to Ishkabibbles to see if Breezy was working. She was one of the few punks they knew with a regular job and she would sometimes sneak them free pizza fries or chili-cheese-dogs when she could, but it was too early. They weren't open yet and Breezy was probably still sleeping off her hangover. For all they knew she might have never left the party. She may have still been back at their house, passed out in one of the bedrooms.

"Damn!"

"I guess we need to walk up to the Gallery."

"Fuck, I really ain't in the mood. You in the mood to starve?"

"Fuck! Let's go."

They left South Street and headed up Fourth Street, trudging through the snow. They'd only walked a few blocks when they spotted a group of skinheads heading down Fourth Street in the opposite direction on the other side of the street. There were six of them. Mack loved those odds.

"Well, things are looking up. Let's cross the street."

Mack was grinning like a kid chasing an ice cream truck.

"Aw, come on, Mack. It's too damn cold to fight."

"I can't help it, Demon. This is what I do. You get money and bitches. I beat the shit out of skinheads!"

Mack stepped out into the street, holding out his hand to stop an oncoming Camaro. Jason paused to let the car pass before he followed. Mack crossed the street in a few long strides and overtook the three skinheads.

"Hey bitches!" Mack said, then lifted his knee to his chest and kicked the first skinhead directly in the face. The man went down, holding his busted nose while his buddies

44

charged. Mack had his attack perfected. He would kick one in the chest to knock him back and buy himself some time while he punched another one. Each punch he threw landed flush on the jaw. He never seemed to miss.

Jason pulled a bike chain from his inside pocket and whipped it hard across one of the skin's legs, dropping him to his knees, howling in pain. He finished him with a combat boot to the side of the guy's head. By the time he turned to face the next one, Mack had already dropped three more. Four of the six skinheads were now lying unconscious on the sidewalk. Jason stepped forward with the chain. The two remaining skinheads raised their fists, ready to fight. One was almost the same height as Mack but twice as wide. He was big but he looked soft. The shorter one looked like a wrestler. His bomber jacket had slipped down off his shoulders, revealing big muscular traps that almost reached his earlobes. He had a tattoo around his neck that read "White Power". There was a swastika tattooed on the back of his hand.

"Put the chain down and fight like a fucking man. We'll take you and your monkey!" the wrestler said.

Mack took off his motorcycle jacket and handed it to Jason.

"I got this, Demon."

Jason took Mack's jacket, draped it over his arm and leaned against one of the parked cars that lined the street. He took out a pack of Kools, tapped the bottom of the pack, then opened it and lit one up, blowing out a smoke ring. He stomped his feet in place, rubbing his belly and looking impatient.

"Make it quick. I'm still fucking hungry."

The first skinhead, the big guy, swung a clumsy right hand that Mack swatted aside like he was fanning away an unpleasant smell. The skinhead's momentum carried him forward, right into Mack's knee. Mack drove it hard into the big guy's chin, smiling maliciously when he heard the satisfying crunch of chattered teeth. The guy dropped to the sidewalk at Mack's feet. Mack stepped over the unconscious skinhead and waved the wrestler forward. The guy with the White Power tattoo was the only one left. He sneered and stepped forward with both fists raised then turned and ran, Mack chased after him.

"Mack! Wait! Fuck!" Jason yelled as he tried to follow them. He ran a few yards then stopped. He was still carrying Mack's coat and it felt like it weighed a ton.

Mack chased the wrestler for two blocks. He hated the idea that a sonuvabitch with the nerve to walk around his town with a swastika and a white power tattoo was going to get away unscathed. Just the thought of it made him want to scream.

"Aaaarrrrrrrrgh! Get back here and fight me, you fucking pussy! Get tha fuck back here!"

Mack's motorcycle boots slipped in the snow and he had to grab hold of a mailbox to keep from falling on his ass. The skinhead stopped and held up both middle fingers.

"Fuck you, nigger! White Power! Unrest!" The wrestler pumped his fist in the air then picked up a bottle and threw it at Mack. It hit him in the forehead and shattered. Blood dribbled down Mack's face into his eyes. The short, muscle-bound skinhead laughed and took off running again. Mack was insane with rage.

"I'm going to tear your fucking heart out!"

Mack pushed himself off the mailbox and tried to chase the guy again. This time he did fall. His legs kicked out from beneath him and he landed hard on his back. He tried to get up and fell down again. Jason caught up with him just as he managed to scramble to his feet.

"You done now?"

Mack turned, every muscle was tensed and for a moment he could see his fist pounding into Jason's face but the kid was just too damned cute to hate. Jason smiled and handed

Mack his jacket. Mack deflated, feeling foolish for what he'd been thinking. He probably did look pretty silly rolling around in the snow. He laughed.

"Yeah, motherfucker. I'm done."

He shrugged back into his jacket and continued walking toward Market Street and the Gallery Mall.

"I think I hurt my hand on one of their thick fucking heads."

"We just took on six skinheads and won. You know what this means, right?"

"It means we're a couple of bad-asses."

"It means that next time they'll bring more. We just made ourselves the number one targets of The Unrest."

"Fuck The Unrest. If I knew where they hung out I'd walk right into their fucking clubhouse and kill every one of those fuckers. I'd burn it down and beat the shit out of anyone who tried to get out. I'd do a fucking Osage on their asses!"

"Mack, I don't think you hear what I'm sayin'. They're gonna be gunnin' for us now."

Mack stopped walking and turned to look Jason in the eyes.

"I hear exactly what you're saying. I just don't give a fuck. They want me? Then they can come get me. I fucking hope they come for me. I'll kill any bitch-ass skinhead who steps to me! They can bring ten, fuck, they can bring twenty motherfuckers! They may get me, but I swear I'll kill a dozen of those motherfuckers first!"

Mack could see the fear in Jason's eyes and he wished he had some words of encouragement but he didn't feel the same fear. The idea of fighting a dozen skinheads excited him. The idea of dying in battle thrilled him. It was how he wanted to die, like a true warrior, going out on his shield. The prospect of living, leaving Philly to go off to college, one day leaving college to get a nine-to-five, having the wife, the house, the car, the kids, the dog, grandkids, winding up in an old folks home getting his adult diaper changed by apathetic nurses, that was far scarier. Getting old terrified him. Dying a legend, was his dream.

At no time in Mack's life had he ever expected to live a long life. The life expectancy for young black males in the 80s was the lowest it had ever been. Every morning that he opened his eyes and breathed fresh air was a surprise to him. He felt like he was living on borrowed time and that was cool. At least now, he knew exactly how he would die. It was a comforting feeling.

"Fuck going all the way to The Gallery. It's too damn cold out here. Let's go over to The Gathering Space. Padre always has coffee and stuff. There might be some donuts and cookies left over from the AA meeting."

"Yeah, it's cold as fuck out here. Let's go see Padre."

FIVE

The Gathering Space, South Street, 11:22AM

Father Antonio ran a small volunteer center out of a second floor storefront above a goth clothing store called "Trash and Vaudeville". He held Alcoholics Anonymous and Narcotics Anonymous meetings there as well as group therapy sessions for runaways and abused kids. A lot of kids hung out there because they always had coffee, it was warm, and Father Antonio never tried to preach to them about Jesus or talk them into going home to their parents. He just listened. He was good at that.

All the kids on South Street called him Padre. No one knew why. Father Antonio was Italian, not Latino. But the name had stuck.

"Hey, Padre!"

"Mack. Jason. You kids stayin' out of trouble?"

"Not if we can help it," Jason replied.

He bumped fists with Padre then took a seat on one of the donated couches. Mack nodded in greeting then sat down beside Jason. Mack liked Padre but he didn't completely trust him. He thought it was weird that the man spent so much time hanging out with teenagers.

"Is there any coffee, Padre?" Jason asked.

It was a rhetorical question. There was always coffee there.

Padre walked into the makeshift kitchen which was little more than a counter with a hotplate and a coffeemaker with two cabinets above it filled with paper plates and Styrofoam cups.

"I heard you two got into a fight?"

Mack and Jason looked at each other in disbelief.

"That was just ten minutes ago. How'd you hear about it already?"

"Lucas, that red-headed kid who looked like he shaved his head with a weed whacker told me. He said he was driving his car down Fourth Street and he saw the two of you fighting ten skinheads. He said you and Mack knocked out ten guys all by yourselves. He said he drove around the block and was going to jump out and help you guys but by the time he got there, the two of you were gone and the skinheads were all lying unconscious on the sidewalk. Is that true?"

Mack looked at Jason and shook his head. Jason smiled. The rumor had begun to grow already. The six skinheads they'd beaten, an incredible feat in of itself, had now become ten via the power of the rumor mill.

"Yeah, it's true. We fucked 'em up!"

"Well, be careful. Those Unrest guys are a bad group. I heard something on the news last night about a few of them being wanted by the police for setting an old black lady on fire at the subway station."

"What?"

"She was seventy-two years old and they burned her alive. It was horrible."

Mack couldn't believe what he was hearing. That could have been his grandmother or one of his great aunts. They were all around that age. *How could anyone do something like that to another human being?*

"Something really needs to be done about them."

Padre leaned forward and put a hand on Mack's shoulder. Mack tensed but allowed it to remain.

"Don't do anything you'll regret, Mack. I know that you were accepted into a good college. Antioch right? You've got a bright future ahead of you. Don't jeopardize all of that fighting with those guys. Most of them are going to wind up in prison or strung out on drugs."

"Or dead," Jason added. He turned to Mack and smiled but looked away when Mack didn't return it. He couldn't understand how Jason could joke about a man's dead body lying in the basement of the house they were squatting in. He still didn't know how they were going to get rid of it.

The front door opened and two girls in leather miniskirts, torn fishnet stockings and leather motorcycle jackets walked in looking like refugees from a Russ Meyers film. One was a tall blonde with shoulder length hair that looked oily and unwashed. She wore dark eyeshadow, black lipstick, and black fingernail polish. She had large lips curled into a sensual sneer. The other was a short black chick with breasts the size of beach balls and a belly to match. Her head was completely shaved and she wore the same dark eye-makeup and lipstick and an almost identical sneer. Her name was Simon and the blonde's name was Cat. They were part-time prostitutes, full-time drug addicts, and regular fixtures around South Street.

"Hello, Simon. Hi, Cat." Padre said, smiling wide.

"Welcome, bitches!" Mack said, climbing from the couch with his arms spread wide.

"Nigga, please!" Simon replied.

They rushed into his arms and Mack kissed them both, long and deep like they were long lost lovers.

"Hey, Padre. Do you mind if we use your restroom?"

"I'm not fucking you here, Mack." Simon chimed in.

"What about you, Cat?"

"I would love to, but it would be weird doing it here."

"Weird is sexy."

"Beatin' the shit out of twenty skinheads is sexy." Cat ran her hand down Mack's chest and down the front of his jeans. She stroked his hardening erection a few times grinning and licking her lips.

"Damn, how the hell did you two hear about that shit

already? It just happened like fifteen minutes ago."

"It's all over the street. You guys are fucking heroes now."

"Well how about a hero's blowjob?"

"Twenty skinheads." Jason laughed.

"I thought there were a dozen of them?" Padre asked.

Jason shrugged.

"We didn't count 'em."

Mack shook his head and turned back to Cat and Simon who were still hugging him. He reached down and rubbed one of Simon's massive tits.

"So, how about that blowjob?"

"Sure. Fuck it."

Mack took the two girls into the bathroom. Father Antonio started to protest.

"Um... this really isn't the place for that... uh... that kind of...."

"Oh, let them have some fun, Padre. What's the harm in it?" Jason said. He stood up and draped an arm over Father Antonio's shoulders.

The bathroom door slammed shut and locked. Father Antonio let out an exasperated sigh. Jason shrugged and winked at him.

"Boys will be boys, Padre. Besides Mack's going through some shit right now. The girl he loves got hurt a couple weeks ago. She's in a coma and he never got the chance to tell her he loves her. He's real fucked up about it."

"Well, I don't think that having sex with other girls is the way to handle it."

Jason shrugged.

"That's how Mack handles it. Is the coffee ready yet?"

SIX

They were walking to Little Davey's house, where they planned to get drunk, listen to music, and watch horror movies on the VCR. *Nightmare On Elm Street* had just come out on VHS. Skinner was singing *Guilty of Being White* by Terrorist Threat at the top of his lungs, irritating the hell out of Bo and Little Davey.

"Man, shut the fuck up!" Bo yelled.

"It's Terrorist Threat, man."

"I hate that song!"

"Why? It's fuckin' awesome!"

"It's too apologetic," Little Davey said.

"Yeah. It's like he's fucking apologizing for being white,"

"That's not what he's saying. It's about how we get blamed for all that shit and people *want* us to apologize."

"And he does. The first words in the song are 'I'm sorry'. Fuck being sorry. I'm proud that my ancestors owned slaves. I wish we still did. Could you imagine if we owned slaves right now? We wouldn't have to do shit. They'd cook for us, clean the apartment. I'd fuck their women just like those niggers are fucking ours now. Why apologize for that? They would have done the same shit to us if they'd been able to. Look how they treated us in school. We were getting our asses kicked everyday because they were the majority. Well, in the real world, we're the fucking majority. Don't apologize for that shit."

"Yeah, that song is weak," Bo said, punching Skinner in the arm.

53

"Ow! Quit playin'! That hurt."

"Quit playin'!" Bo mocked.

"I still like the song."

"That's cause you're a pussy." Bo punched him in the arm again,

"Quit it, dude!"

Little Davey walked up to Skinner and poked him in the chest. "Bo is right. That song is weak. You want to be a skinhead, you need to sing something with balls, like *Skrewdriver*."

"Fuckin' A! Like *The Way It's Gotta Be*! That song fuckin' Rocks! Bo began bellowing the lyrics at the top of his lungs. Little Davey joined in, shouting the lyrics in Skinner's face along with flecks of spittle.

With obvious reluctance, Skinner joined in. They bumped chests and high-fived.

"Fuckin' A, dude. That's real music!" Bo said, grinning from ear to ear.

"Let's play kick the cat," Little Davey said, smiling mischievously.

A small calico crossed the sidewalk in front of them and, true to his word, Little Davey stepped forward and kicked it, catching it in the ribs and lifting it off the ground into the air and into the street, into traffic. A small Subaru struck it and knocked it into the gutter. It lay there, bleeding from the ears and mouth, its tail twitching spastically. Davey wanted to watch it die but didn't want his friends to think he was weird. He laughed as the cat made a hissing sound that slowly wound down like a punctured tire. When he turned to look at his friends, their expressions were completely horrified.

Too late. They already think I'm weird.

"That wasn't funny, man. I like cats," Bo said.

"Yeah, dude. Not cool," Skinner said.

"Fuck you, Skinner! Does Bo know how you got your nickname?"

Skinner blushed.

"Just chill, dude."

"Chill? You sound like a fucking nigger."

"How did you get your nickname?" Bo asked. "I always thought Skinner was your last name or your middle name or something."

They stopped walking and Little Davey turned around, not just to face Bo, but also so that he'd have a good view of the dying cat in the gutter in back of them.

"This mick? His last name is McDowell. Evan McDowell. Everyone calls him Skinner because when he was a kid he used to torture animals, skin them alive and shit, *including* fucking cats. His mom sent him away for a whole summer, to a mental hospital." Little Davey turned to Skinner and sneered. "Now, what? You're some kind of fucking animal lover or something? What? Did they cut your balls off in the loony bin?"

Skinner looked like his face was boiling. Tears squeezed out from the corners of his eyes. He was breathing hard and bouncing up and down on his toes. His fingers curled into fists.

"What? You want to hit me now, Skinner? You want to kick my ass? Go ahead. Go ahead and hit me, psycho! I promise you that you'll know exactly what those animals felt like if you do." Davey pulled a large Bowie knife from under his jacket and waved it in Skinner's face. "Cause I'll cut all the skin, the muscle, and the fat off your bones. I won't just skin you, psycho. I'll fucking fillet your ass!"

Bo stepped between them.

"Cut it out, guys. We don't fight each other. You're acting like a bunch of ghetto scum right now. Save that shit for the porch monkeys."

Little Davey tucked his knife back into his jacket and held his hands up in surrender.

"Okay, Bo. I'll *chill*," he said derisively.

"So, what are we gonna do today? You want to head

into Philly and hang out on South Street? I heard *Suicidal Tendencies* is playing at Club Revival with *Terrorist Threat* I love that band. They're fucking hardcore!"

Bo and Skinner looked at each other.

"You didn't hear?" Bo asked.

"Hear what?"

"All the punk kids in Philly have declared war on us. A bunch of skins got jumped at *Pizzaz* last Sunday at a *Murphy's Law* concert. They were playing with *Agnostic Front* and a couple local bands, *Uncivil Disobedience* or somebody. The place was full of punks and straight-edge kids and some of our Unrest brothers. Anyway, some black guys from the projects showed up with some punk kids from South Street and started a big riot. A lot of our boys got hurt bad. Oh, and these two punk kids beat up like twenty skinheads on South Street this morning."

Little Davey looked like he was about to explode.

"Two fucking punks beat up twenty skinheads?"

"Yeah, one of them was this big black kid named Mack. I think he knows karate or something. Todd, you know that muscle-head jock from the football team? He was with them and his punk ass ran. Left all his brothers behind."

Little Davey looked like he'd just been slapped and spit on.

"Fucking karate? That's bullshit! Why didn't anybody tell me about this shit? Why haven't we had a meeting?"

Bo and Skinner looked at the floor.

"There was a meeting. We went to get you, but...uh... Big Dave, I mean ... uh ... your dad was drunk and chased us off your porch. We tried to call too, but no one answered."

Little Davey began pacing back and forth on the sidewalk. He rubbed his face with both hands, kicked a hole in a wooden fence then turned and kicked a dent in a parked car with his steel-toed Doc Martins, imagining that it was a punk rocker's head.

"So, what the fuck was said at the meeting?"

"John Jones ordered everybody to stay out of Philly until after Christmas."

"And then?"

Bo lit up. He nodded his head enthusiastically, licking his lips and punching his fist into his palm.

"There's a Skanking Razor concert the night before new Year's Eve. We're all going down there together and we're going to fuck all those punks up. He's put a five-hundred dollar bounty on that kid Mack," Bo said.

"I hate those *Skanking Razor* pussies," Skinner added.

"Yeah, we all do. And they all know it. That's why all the punks will be there to protect them, but they won't be expecting a hundred of us to show up at once. We'll fuck their asses up!" Bo said, punching his fist into his palm again.

Little Davey looked up at the sky as if imploring God for help in dealing with his two idiot friends. He ran both hands down his face again and let out a long sigh.

"Not if there's two hundred of 'em! We'll be the ones getting fucked up. Again!"

He paused and stared at the ground, pacing back and forth and flexing his fingers as if strangling something. He grit his teeth. His nostrils flared. A large vein popped out on his forehead and pulsated. It looked like it was about to rupture.

"We should bring guns."

Bo shook his head. "John said no guns. If we start shooting then they'll start shooting and then the cops'll get involved and we'll all wind up dead or in jail. No guns."

"A fucking kid beats up twenty of our brothers and his solution is to bring a hundred? And this time there won't be just one or two guys. They'll be like a hundred, two hundred of 'em! I'm bringing a gun. My dad has an old .45 Smith and Wesson. I'm bringing it with me. And I'm killing that singer from *Skanking Razor* too. Those sons of bitches started all this shit with their lyrics about bashing skinheads. They need to die too."

"Why not kill all the guys from *Camper Van Beethoven* too?" Bo said. "They wrote that song *Take The Skinheads Bowling* that all those fucking hardcore kids sing. I bet that's inspired a few of 'em to go after us. Why not kill them too then?"

Little Davey sneered and nodded his head in agreement.

"If those bastards were gonna be there I'd shoot them too."

"You're crazy," Bo said, pointing at Little Davey.

"No way, man. I ain't killing nobody," Skinner said. "They'll put me back in an institution. I ain't going back there."

"I don't care. We can't let the niggers and Jews think that we're scared of 'em. We can't let 'em think we're weak. Did you know that most punk rockers are Jews? It's a fact! And now there are nigger and spic punks too. They're all joining forces against the pure white man. That's what's happening out there. My dad may be a piece of shit but he's a hardworking American. Not like these fucking mud people who come over here and leech off society, stealing and scamming and taking welfare instead of getting fucking jobs. And when they do get a job, they don't know enough to charge a decent wage so they work for shit wages which makes it hard for a white man to make a decent living. The fucking spics are taking all the damn jobs because they'll work for the price of a taco. Meanwhile, the niggers are fucking all the white women and selling drugs to our kids. Look at who our women idolize now. You go into any teenage girl's room in America and she'll have a poster of Prince or Michael-fucking-Jackson. That's what's happening to our white women, all over the country. They're growing up being taught to lust after black men. We let 'em win this time and this shit will just get worse. They'll take over the whole fucking country! My dad is right about that much. How do you think it looks that those fuckin' punks are kickin' our asses? Everyone's probably talking about it! They're laughing at us right now!"

Little Davey's dad was a painter by trade. He used to charge fourteen dollars an hour to paint a house until Mexicans and Puerto Ricans started undercutting him. Now, if he wanted to work, he could barely charge more than seven dollars an hour without being outbid and losing the job. That was just barely enough to pay the bills and not nearly enough to support his growing alcohol addiction. The worse things got economically, the more he'd taken it out on his young son. Black eyes and busted lips had been regular sights on Little Davey's face for as long as Bo and Skinner had known him. Davey's mother left when he was ten after one too many beatings from his drunken father. She promised to come back for him but his dad threatened to kill her if she ever came near his son. He never saw her again. His father told him that his mother had left them for a black man.

"All those fucking jiggaboos are taking our white women. It's happening everywhere I look. That's what happened to your mom. She fell in love with black cock!"

True or not, Little Davey believed it and soon adopted his father's hatred of all things not white. He alienated himself from the few black and Latino friends he had in school and then did the same with his Jewish friends. It wasn't long before he was recruited by *The Unrest* who cultivated his hatred and turned it into an obsession, a personal crusade.

"Don't worry about it. City Gardens has a show coming up this weekend with *Agnostic Front* and *The Circle Jerks*. All those punks from Philly will be there. We'll get their asses then," Bo said, flexing his fat-covered muscles.

"What night? Friday or Saturday?"

"This Friday. Tomorrow night."

"You think those punks will come to Jersey for the show?"

"For *The Circle Jerks*? They'll come. They love that band. Plus, they know we'll be there and they think they can kick our asses now."

"Hey, look at that guy in the Michael Jackson jacket! He looks just like the guy," Bo said, pointing to a guy in black pleather pants, a red pleather jacket with zippers all over it, wearing a white glove and dark sunglasses. His hair was permed so that it was curly and slicked back. He wasn't black. He could have been either Jewish or Italian. Little Davey didn't care. He was in a bad mood and this guy was in the wrong place at the wrong time.

"Faggot!"

He ran across the street and confronted the guy.

"Hey Faggot!"

"I ain't no –"

He never got a chance to finish the words. Little Davey shoved the Bowie knife into his gut so hard that the tip protruded from his back. He pulled it out and slammed it into his chest. The Michael Jackson wannabe crumpled to the pavement. Davey kicked him in the face, sending a spray of blood and teeth into the street. He kicked him in the temple and the guy began to convulse. Several cars screeched to a halt.

"Hey! Leave that kid alone!" a fat guy in his thirties shouted, stepping from his Ford Taurus brandishing a steering wheel lock, ironically named "The Club".

"Fuck you!" Bo yelled back and confronted the guy with nothing but his fists. The guy swung and cracked Bo on the side of the head with The Club. Bo dropped to his knees, shook his head once, then charged, tackling the guy in the middle of the street. While they struggled, Skinner ran over and began stomping the good Samaritan in the face.

"Let's go before the cops come! Stop fucking around you two!" Little Davey yelled. More cars stopped and people were starting to leave their vehicles, yelling and threatening.

Davey pulled Bo off of the motorist and pushed Skinner away.

"Let's fucking GO!"

"This son of a bitch hit me! I'll kill him!"

"Bo! We have to go before the cops get here!"

Bo looked around at the other motorists who were now closing in on them, shouting and pointing at them. One of them was kneeling down next to the Michael Jackson wannabe that Davey stabbed. Skinner had already started running.

"Oh, shit. Did you kill that guy?" Bo whispered.

"Let's just get the fuck out of here," Little Davey said. He started running and Bo quickly followed. A few people in the crowd chased after them. Davey wanted to turn around and use the blade on them. That would teach them. Instead he pumped his fist into the air.

"WHITE POWEEEEERRRRRR!"

In his head, the lyrics to an old *Unrest* song, *Homicidal Maniacs*, played. He shouted them at the top of his lungs as they cut down an alley onto the next street.

"Death is born within the sound!

Now fills the air from town to town!

The hunger grows more every day!

THE MANIAC HAS COME TO PLAY!"

They ran a few more blocks then stopped outside Bo's apartment building.

"I guess we're crashing with you tonight, Bo. We need to stay off the street."

"Damn. My girl is going to have a fucking fit."

"Is she coming over tonight?" Skinner asked.

"Yeah, I was supposed to take her to dinner. It's some kind of anniversary or some shit. Our first kiss, our first fuck, the first time I finger-banged her, fuck if I know. Who the hell can keep up with this shit?"

"Is Lisa coming with her?" Skinner asked.

"I wasn't planning a fucking threesome if that's what you mean."

"Damn, shame. Lisa has some amazing tits," Little Davey chimed in. "I'd love to fuck her myself."

"Be careful. Skinner thinks he's in love with her," Bo said as he fished in his pocket for his keys. He opened the door and they all stepped into the small foyer. Moments later three police cars sped past with sirens blaring.

Skinner blushed then changed the subject, looking back out at the street.

'That was fucking close! Do you think that faggot is dead?" Skinner asked.

Davey shrugged.

"If he ain't dead, he sure as shit ain't happy. That'll teach him to walk around Camden dressed like a fucking queer. *No apparent motive. Just kill and kill again!*" They were the lyrics to a song by Slayer called *"Kill Again"*. Bo and Skinner looked at each other. Their faces showed obvious concern with Davey's choice of songs. That was two people Little Davey murdered in the last week and they were accomplices in both.

The elevator doors opened and the three boys stepped inside. More police cars raced through the neighborhood. Soon they would be coming for them.

Let them come, Davey thought. He fingered the hilt of the bowie knife in his inner pocket. Blood had seeped through the lining of his bomber jacket and saturated his long-sleeved thermal shirt. The elevator doors closed and Davey closed his eyes, reliving the moment when he'd plunge the knife into that faggot. It had been an incredible rush. He'd felt unstoppable, the same way he felt in a mosh pit when *Uncivil Disobedience* or *Skrewdriver* was onstage, like he couldn't be hurt, couldn't be moved, couldn't be resisted!

Let them come.

SEVEN

Market Street, 1:57 pm

The Jersey girls were in the backseat as Jason drove their Suzuki Samurai to the Gallery.

"I don't know about this. My mom will kill me if something happens to this jeep."

"Don't worry about it. We'll bring it right back. We just need to run a quick errand. We'll drop you off at the mall and then pick you up in an hour. That'll give you time to shop."

The skinny girl who stroked Mack's cock when she was trippin', raised her hands, palms up and shrugged.

"We spent all of our money," She wore crystals around her neck and a tie-dyed t-shirt underneath a brown, leather bomber jacket. She looked more like a confused hippy than a punk.

"Well, you can window shop. Pick out all the things you're gonna buy when you come back down this weekend."

"Okay, but just an hour, right?"

Jason smiled as he watched the three girls step out of the jeep. Mack knew that smile. It was an expression of pure mischief but in this case, the mischief had already been done.

"Yeah, right. One hour, max."

The hippie-punk leaned back into the Suzuki and whispered into Mack's ear.

"I would have sucked your dick if my friends weren't here. I think you're fucking hot. Maybe next time." She shrugged, kissed Mack on the cheek, and smiled then rushed to catch up with her friends.

"See, they're not all afraid of the soul pole."

63

Mack smiled then remembered what they were about to do and the smile fell hard from his face, shattering into a dozen lines of worry. Jason popped a cassette tape into the tape deck and turned up the volume. *Public Enemy's* "*Fight The Power*" blared from the speakers. Mack smirked, watching the waifish punk with the vampire-white skin and the haunted eyes rap at the top of his lungs. He looked out the window at the shoppers and commuters rushing to and fro as they passed Chestnut Street, wishing he was amongst them instead of on his way to hide a body. His mood grew increasingly solemn until the song switched to Super Lover Cee and Casanova Rud titled "*Girl's Act Stupid-aly.*"

"Seriously, man? I'm black and I don't even like that shit."

"Super Lover Cee? He's dope!"

"He's fuckin' dumb. Girls act stupid-aly? That's whack. Put some Ministry on."

"Yeah, dude. Stigmata!"

Jason popped one cassette out of the deck and deftly slammed in another. The two cruised the remaining blocks singing about how the look in your eyes was like a car crash or a knife.

"Stigmata!"

Mack pounded the dashboard with his fists and stomped the floorboards as they sang. He loved this song. It was like rocket fuel to him. It made his blood surge with adrenaline. They pulled up in front of the house just as the song ended. Mack stepped out of the Suzuki feeling like a new man.

"Okay, let's do this shit."

He pulled out his keys and unlocked the front door. The air inside felt stale, dry, lifeless. The house was empty for once. The silence was appropriately funereal. Mack and Jason stepped over the blankets, clothes, and fast food wrappers and empty beer bottles and cans as they crept through the house. They didn't speak and they tried hard not to make a sound, tip-toeing like they were afraid to wake the dead. The basement door was still closed.

Mack reached out for the door. His hand trembled with a superstitious dread. He almost expected the door to yank open from the inside and Billy to be standing there with his bleeding head lolling to one side, his neck broken and twisted, but the doorway was dark and empty. He reached inside, still expecting to feel a cold clammy hand clamp over his as he groped for the light switch. He'd seen far too many horror movies. That was practically all he watched. And the only books he read were either by Stephen King, Clive Barker, or Skipp and Spector.

Found it.

He flicked on the light and there was Billy, still lying in the same position he'd been in last night. He was definitely dead.

"Fuck."

He and Jason walked down the stairs. A rat scurried away from the body as they neared the bottom.

"Aw shit. I think that rat was eating on him."

Jason swallowed hard.

"Did it eat his face? Can you see?" He sounded almost excited.

Mack leaned over the corpse to get a better look at his face.

"Naw. He looks fine. Grab an arm."

Mack reached down and grabbed one of Billy's cold dead arms and Jason knelt down and grabbed the other. Rigor mortis had already come and gone and now Billy's body was cold and limp.

"Ewww, man. He feels nasty."

Mack sighed heavily.

"He's dead. How do you expect him to feel?"

"You mad at me, Mack?"

"Naw. We cool. I just want this shit over with."

Jason nodded then looked Mack in the eyes.

"Seriously, dude. I know this shit was my fault. If we get caught, I'll tell them I did it. I'm not gonna let you go down for this. You've got college and shit to worry about."

Mack nodded solemnly.

"Let's just not get caught. Okay?"

"Okay, dude."

The skinhead's corpse was awkward and heavy. Carrying him up the stairs was like carrying a one hundred and sixty pound sack of laundry. Mack lost his balance several times as they dragged Billy up to the living room. He was afraid that all three of them would slip and tumble down the stairs and there would be three bodies for someone to dispose of.

Finally, they made it to the top of the stairs. They were both out of breath.

"Fuck! This sonuvabitch was heavy and he stinks like shit."

"Corpses void their bowels when they die."

"How do you know that?" Jason asked.

Mack shrugged.

"I read a lot."

"Dude, you read some scary shit."

"Yeah, I like horror. It's the only thing that keeps me interested."

"Who? Like Stephen King?"

"Stephen King, Clive Barker, Robert R. McCammon, Skipp and Spector. They're fucking awesome, man. I love their shit."

"I bet you'd dig reading Baudelaire or Comte De Lautremonte."

"Who are they?"

"Poets, dude. Lautremonte wrote this twisted book about satanism and shit called *Les Chants de Maldoror*. The guys from Skinny Puppy said it influenced their music."

"That's cool. I ain't into *Satanism*. I think it's a bunch of bullshit, but I like Skinny Puppy. I'll have to check it out."

"You'd dig it. Seriously."

"Hopefully I won't be reading the shit from prison. Let's get this motherfucker out of here."

"How we gonna get Billy outside to the car without anybody seeing us? Maybe we should have waited until tonight." Jason asked.

"There's too many people hanging around here at night and we won't have a car. Let's just carry him out. Check to make sure there's nobody on the street and just carry him right out the front door. Anyone looking out the window will just think he's drunk."

"We should take off his jacket and put a hat on him or something. We can put his jacket back on when we dump him. It would just be kind of suspicious if the cops report a bald guy in a leather jacket found dead in the projects and some neighbor saw us carrying a bald guy in a leather jacket out of our house."

Mack nodded.

"True. Good idea. There's a beanie over there by the fireplace, on the mantel. Grab one of Rachel's sweatshirts too. We can take it off of him and put the jacket back on 'em when we get to the projects."

They laid Billy down in the living room and stripped off his jacket, slid on a Temple University sweatshirt and a knit cap to cover his bald bloodied head, then picked him up again. Mack carried him under the arms and Jason held his legs.

"Wait. We can't carry him outside like this. It looks like we're carrying a body. We're going to have to get on either side of him."

Jason ran around to the side and through one of the deadman's arms over his shoulder and wrapped his arm around Billy's back, holding him up by the arm pit. He grabbed Billy's belt with his other hand, Mack readjusted his grip to similar hold and they dragged him out the front door. The front steps were slippery and Jason stumbled almost immediately but somehow managed to hold onto Billy.

"Don't drop him. Then he'll really look dead."

Jason shrugged.

"I'm sure the neighbors'll just think he's drunk like everybody else they see coming in and out of here."

The street was empty. Mack kept a close eye on the windows to see if anyone was peeking out and spying on them but he didn't notice anything. Everything looked quiet.

"Here. You drive," Jason said, handing Mack the keys.

"I can't drive."

"Why not?"

"Because I can't drive. I never learned."

"Seriously?"

"Cars are just a waste of money and natural resources. I can get home on the subway, the trolley, the bus, the L train, or the train. Fuck do I need a car for? To drive it to the train station?"

"Okay, just open the door and hand me the keys back. I can't open the door and hold him up too."

Mack opened the back door and they slid Billy in. He handed the keys back to Jason and walked around to the passenger side.

"I wish this thing had tinted windows."

"Maybe we should close his eyelids," Jason said.

Mack looked back at Billy's face, seeing it for the first time. His eyes were wide open and his eyeballs looked wrinkly and deflated. His eyeball rather. One of them was missing. There was just a huge ragged orifice where it had been.

"That fucking rat ate his damn eyeball!"

He reached back and closed Billy's eyelids.

"This is about the craziest fucking thing I've ever done. I'm getting seriously fucked up when this is over."

"Me too," Jason said.

68

They drove toward Eleventh Street, toward Creative and Performing Arts High School where they'd both met. CAPA was right next to the Martin Luther King Housing Projects. There was an empty lot beside the projects filled with trash, old furniture, rusted out cars, and illegally dumped building materials. They were sure they could dump the body there easily without being seen. It was Friday, so the usual gaggle of unwashed ashy-kneed kids who played in the lot would still be in school. As long as there weren't any homeless people there picking through the garbage they would be fine.

Minutes after leaving the house, they drove past their old school. Mack looked up at the five story building and a feeling of sadness descended on him as he remembered all the high hopes he'd had for himself when he was first accepted into CAPA. He thought he'd be the next Stephen King. He expected to write his first horror novel before his senior year and become one of the world's youngest bestselling authors. He'd started a novel but never came close to finishing it and now, he was a murderer.

"I'm going home for a bit after this, Demon. I just need a few hours to myself, to lay low and get my head straight. I still want to go to that concert Friday night at City Gardens if you can get us a ride. *The Circle Jerks* are playing. I just need to workout, say hi to my mom, get something to eat, and get some rest. It's been a crazy ass day. We'll hook up tomorrow night though."

Jason was silent. Mack knew his friend hated it when he left, but Mack still had a home. He didn't hate his parents like the rest of them. He loved his mom. He just loved the streets too. He loved the scene.

"I'll be back tomorrow night, Demon. I promise."

"Yeah, okay. It's cool, dude. Hey, but would you mind coming to my house with me? They might let me in if you're with me. My parents hate starting shit when company is around."

Mack nodded.

"Of course, man. No problem. I got your back."

The Martin Luther King Housing Project's three twelve story tenement buildings towered above them as they pulled into the adjacent lot. They were quiet as projects go. At this hour of the day, there was very little activity. Somehow, in broad daylight, it didn't seem quite so dangerous. It just seemed sad.

The residents who had jobs were still at work, many on their second or third job in the last twenty four hours. Those who were unemployed were still out looking for work, hustling up money for food or bills or drug money, or still asleep. Old ladies scurried about, shopping or doing laundry. Young mothers pushed strollers or carried infants on their hips, gossiping amongst themselves and yelling threats at their young children. Soon the older kids would be getting out of school or coming back from wherever they'd gone instead of school. That's when it was best not to be there if you didn't belong. In the projects, anyone over the age of eight was likely to be armed and dangerous.

There was a police substation directly across the street which kept the usual violence contained if not at all minimized. Mack and Jason eyed it warily as they drove around to the far end of the vacant lot where one of the tenement buildings would block their view of the substation and likewise block the substation's view of them. There was a large pile of cinderblocks and broken furniture in the farthest corner by a chain link fence.

"Let's dump him over there."

Jason pulled the Suzuki alongside the piles of trash and debris so that the vehicle would partially shield them from anyone who happened to be on the street. They lifted a torn, rodent infested, plaid couch and scooted aside an old piss-stained mattress and a few cinder blocks to make a hole in the pile of trash big enough for a body.

"Let's do this quick and get the fuck out of here. Grab his legs."

Jason jerked Billy out of the car by his legs then Mack grabbed him under the arms and tossed him onto the mound of debris. They piled the mattress and couch on top of him. Without digging through trash and lifting the furniture, no one would find him. At least not until he began to smell.

"Let's go."

EIGHT

Jason's house, 2:16 pm

Architecturally, Jason's house was almost identical to the one Mack had grown up in. but it was about a hundred years newer. It had been painted within the last decade. The front door and the windows had likewise been replaced in the last ten years. The front steps were made of red brick rather than concrete and they weren't cracked and crumbling like those at Mack's house. Even the iron railing was ornate and freshly powder-coated. Inside, the differences were even greater.

The furniture was modern and matching. All the kitchen and dining room chairs matched. The tables didn't wobble and there were no matchbooks or popsicle sticks shoved under them to balance them. The sofa matched the loveseat which matched the lounge chairs which matched the coffee table which matched the end tables which matched the walls which matched the carpeting. Everything in the house was perfectly coordinated. It made Mack uncomfortable. He felt like the only thing in the entire house that didn't match. Even Jason fit in some odd way. Mack couldn't see how his presence could possibly help.

Jason's stepfather, Melvin Sadler, was a pathetic excuse for a man. He was soft around the middle. His arms and legs were thin and completely devoid of muscle tone. He looked almost womanly. His thinning hair was heavily moussed and looked like far too much time had been spent on the styling of it. His nails were manicured and his pajamas looked too expensive. Mack knew the man was not half as well-to-do as he pretended to be. It was no secret that he had put the family heavily in debt. He liked to act like he was a big shot real estate guy. But the reality was that his big sales were few and far between. In between sales, he lived off credit.

Beside Mister Sadler, Jason's mom fretted, wringing her hands and huffing her dissatisfaction. Her child, her creation, had rebelled. He had escaped her control. It was something she could not understand and was ill-equipped to cope with. Her chubby face was a maze of worry lines.

"I just want to spend the night in my own bed, Mom."

"Do you have a job yet?" his stepfather asked. "And weren't you supposed to be going to college, Mack? Don't tell me you gave up a real chance at a successful future to hang out with this clown."

Jason bristled, preparing to lash out and Mack put a hand on his shoulder, both to hold him back and to console him. He knew that Jason wanted to punch his father in his smug little mouth as badly as he did, but it only would have made things worse.

"No, sir. I'm still going to college. I just deferred my enrollment for a year. There's some things I need to take care of here first."

"What could be more important than college?"

"Mom! Would you do something? That's none of his business! Don't interrogate him."

Jason's stepfather held his hands up.

"I'm sorry if I overstepped my boundaries. I just hate to see promising young people throwing their lives away."

Mack smiled mirthlessly.

"I'm not, Melvin. Life is good."

Melvin Sadler wrinkled his eyebrows in an expression stuck somewhere between confusion, amusement, and anger, unsure whether or not Mack was being some kind of smartass and fucking with him. Mack continued to smile until Mr. Sadler looked away.

"So, can I stay?"

"Sure, baby," his mother finally spoke up. "But I can't give you any money. I don't want you getting drunk."

"I don't want any money. I'll be right back. I have to drop Mack off at the train station and return the car."

Mack reached out and shook Mr. and Mrs. Sadler's hands.

"Good to see you again, Mrs. Sadler. Thanks for the advice, Melvin."

They turned and walked out the door.

Jason started laughing as soon as the door closed.

"Oh my god, dude! I almost lost it when you called him Melvin. He hates when kids call him by his first name."

Mack sneered.

"I know. But I ain't no fuckin' kid no more. I just wanted him to remember that shit. You let his ass know that if he hits you or anything, I'm gonna kick his fuckin' ass. Let's take the girls their jeep back."

Jason shook his head, still chuckling.

"Dude. You're a trip. That's why I love you. You've always got my back."

"I love you too, man."

NINE

Arch Street, in back of The Gallery Mall, 3:03 pm

The Jersey girls were a little upset when Mack and Jason showed up late with the Suzuki. They were even angrier because the vehicle stank and there were red, yellow, and brown stains on the back seat.

"Did somebody take a shit in my car?" Sharon, a redheaded girl in a pink ski jacket, said. It was her vehicle and she did not look amused.

The body must have still been leaking fluids when they put him back there and some of Billy's putrescence had leaked out onto the upholstery.

"Were you wearing that pink coat when we met you?" Jason asked, laughing. "It makes you look preppy."

"Demon had a little bit of a hangover from last night. He threw up back there. We'll clean it up."

"No! Just stay the fuck away from my car. We've got to go. I'll clean it up when we get back across the bridge."

Great. We're leaving evidence everywhere.

Sharon was still scowling and wrinkling up her nose.

"I can't believe you threw up in my Samurai. It smells like shit back there!"

Jason smiled demurely and gave them his wounded puppy look.

"I'm really, sorry. I wasn't feeling well. We'll clean it up for you."

"No. No. We've got to get home."

Mack tried his best not to look concerned. The Suzuki smelled like something died in it. To Mack, it smelled like a guilty verdict, like death row, like a lethal injection. He didn't know how he and Jason hadn't noticed it before.

The hippie-punk who'd flirted with Mack earlier, smiled at him as the three girls climbed into the Suzuki. Mack didn't return the smile. Pussy was the last thing on his mind. He felt bad that one of the girls had to sit in the back with the corpse feces smeared into the seat beside them. But he felt worse imagining one of them complaining about the smell then finding out that Billy disappeared the same day that they borrowed the vehicle and then finding out that he'd turned up dead and they'd brought the Suzuki back stained with brown and red smears that could have been blood or shit or some combination of the two and putting two and two together. If this had been a movie, Mack would have killed all three girls and burned the vehicle. Instead, he watched them drive away. His head hurt and his stomach felt like it had a pinwheel spinning inside it tipped with razorblades.

He turned around and staggered back into the mall toward the train station, feeling like he was taking that long walk toward the execution chamber. Jason was saying something to him, laughing and joking in a nervous way that let Mack know that he was scared too, but Mack couldn't hear exactly what the kid was saying over the defining sound of a judge's gavel pounding the bench and a prison door slamming shut.

Mack hugged Jason goodbye then walked down to the train station below the Gallery Mall, alone.

"Be careful, Demon. "

"You too, Big Mack. Don't worry about all this. Everything'll be fine. Nobody gives a damn about a dead skinhead."

"Yeah. I'll see you tomorrow night."

TEN

Bo's apartment, 5:34 pm

"We're out of beer. Out of movies. There's nothing on TV. I can't stay here anymore," Little Davey said.

"But you said we were going to stay here all night, until the heat goes down."

Little Davey shook his head.

"It's been almost six hours. They ain't lookin' for us no more. Besides, Bo and his girl want some alone time. She's lookin' at me like she wants to kill me. If we break out now they might still be able to make it to that restaurant."

Gia smiled for the first time since she walked through the door. Gia Milano was a short, skinny, Italian from Atlantic City with a remarkably beautiful face but no tits or ass to speak of. She wore a tight white miniskirt and black fishnet stockings with high-heeled boots and a white ski-coat with fur around the color. Her hair was permed and blow-dried so that it had twice its normal volume. Her bangs were flipped up in front and hair sprayed in place. She wore bright blue eyeshadow, pink blush and candy apple red lipstick. Davey thought she looked like a fucking clown.

"Yeah, you guys will be fine. Davey's right."

"Like you fucking care," Skinner said. "You just want to get to your stupid anniversary dinner. You don't give a fuck if we both get arrested as long as you get to go to Red Lobster or wherever the fuck."

"I'm going. I've got to see my kid," Davey said, turning to leave.

"You've got a kid?" Gia asked.

77

"You didn't know that? He's got a son." Bo answered, speaking up for the first time as he crushed a beer can, the last Budweiser in the house.

"Who's the mother?" Gia asked, looking both curious and disgusted at the thought of the psycho little skinhead playing daddy to an impressionable little kid.

"You remember Cindy Singer? That girl he used to be all in love with? She had a kid last year. She found out she was pregnant right after they broke up. Ain't that fucked up?"

"Damn. How old was she? Wasn't she like seventeen or something? She was still in high school."

"I'm outta here," Little Davey said. He didn't like the tone of the conversation. No one had said anything negative yet but there was a tone in Gia's voice that was pissing him off. Any minute she was going to let her tongue slip and say something bad about him being a father. He didn't know if he'd be able to control himself if that happened. He'd hate to lose Bo as a friend because he had to gut the man's girlfriend.

"I'm stayin' right here," Skinner said, crossing his arms and leaning back on the tattered couch.

"Fuck if you are, dude! If Davey can leave then so can you!" Bo stood up and grabbed Skinner's jacket. He handed it to him then walked over to the front door and opened it.

Skinner looked like he was about to cry.

"Dude, you're sending me right into the arms of the police. They're going to put me on death row!"

Bo rolled his eyes and raised his arms in a gesture of surrender.

"Fuckin' A, dude! Get off the cross. You'll be fine. Just take side streets and alleys if you're scared."

Skinner's bottom lip trembled and his eyes watered as he took his jacket from Bo and shuffled out the door after Little Davey.

"Have fun, guys," Davey said, heading for the stairwell.

"Thanks, man. Call me if anything happens. Okay?"

"We'll be fine," Davey replied.

"First degree murder if we get caught. That's the death penalty, dude. For *all* of us."

Little Davey stopped in his tracks and turned to face Skinner. His face had turned red and that vein was pulsating in his forehead the way it did when he was really mad.

"What the fuck does that mean, Skinner?"

Skinner looked down at his ox-blood combat boots, shuffling from one foot to the other.

"I'm just sayin' that we're all in this together."

"Really? Is that what you're saying? Cause it sounds like you're threatening to rat us out if you get caught. Is that what you mean by us being in this together, Skinner?"

Bo was still standing in the doorway watching. Skinner turned his head to look up the hallway at Bo and took a few involuntary steps backwards. When he turned back to Little Davey, he already looked like he was preparing to run. Davey slid his hand in his jacket where he kept his knife. Skinner swallowed hard and his eyes watered.

"Uh... n-no, man. You know I wouldn't drop the dime on you guys."

Little Davey stared at Skinner for a long tense moment, his hand still in his jacket on the hilt of his knife. He was thinking that if he killed the guy right here it would put Bo in a bad spot. He didn't think Bo would squeal, but that dago bitch of his certainly would. Killing someone you knew was never smart. You always got caught for shit like that. If you wanted to get away with murder, it had to be random. He'd learned that reading all those Ann Rule crime books. He pulled his hand out of his pocket and shook his head.

"Fuckin' drop the dime? Why are you always talking like that? Drop the dime. White guys don't talk like that. If you want to be black so bad then go ahead and move to the fuckin' ghetto with the rest of the jiggaboos. See how long your white ass would last."

Behind him, Bo laughed. "Yeah, you thought high school was bad."

"I- I don't talk like a black dude."

Little Davey smiled malevolently and pointed his finger at Skinner like it was a gun.

"I'll see you later, Skinner. You stay out of trouble."

Davey turned his back and walked down the hall. He had a bad feeling about the next few days and he wanted to see his kid before anything bad happened to any of them. He had a suspicion that this might be his last opportunity.

His ex-girlfriend lived in the neighborhood. Davey walked three blocks down to the WAWA food market on the corner. He stopped at a pay phone in the parking lot of the WAWA to call Cindy, just to make sure she was home and that she didn't have a guy in there with her. If that bitch had some dude in there with his kid he didn't know what he'd do. He fished around his pockets and found a quarter, thinking again how stupid that saying "drop the dime was". *When was the last time a damn phone call was only a dime? It should be drop the damn quarter.* Cindy answered on the fourth ring.

"Hello?"

"Cindy? It's Davey. Look, I want to come see Mickey."

There was a long pause and a sigh.

"Did you hear me? I said I want to see my son!"

"Why do you want to see him?"

"He's my son."

Another long pause.

"He needs diapers."

"I just gave you money for diapers and baby food."

"That was a week ago. Babies use a lot of diapers."

Davey pulled out his wallet. It was empty. He punched the side of the phone booth.

"Yeah, okay. I'll get 'em some more diapers."

"I need money to buy him some more clothes too. He's

almost outgrown everything he's got."

"Yeah, yeah. I said I'd get you some more money. Now, can I see my kid?"

She sighed again. The sound made Davey want to smash the phone in her face. He gritted his teeth and struggled to keep his anger in check. If he flipped out on her, she'd never let him see his kid and, despite his flaws, Little Davey loved his son.

From the moment Mikey was born Little Davey was surprised by the depth and immediacy of his love for his boy. He'd been born via caesarean. Davey held Cindy's hand as the doctors cut her open then stuck their hands inside her, up to the elbows, fishing for Mikey who kept squirming away from them. By the time they grabbed his legs and dragged him out, Cindy had lost a massive amount of blood. They were still stitching her up and talking about the possibility of giving her a few units of blood when the nurses finished suctioning the blood and amniotic fluid from the baby's ears, nose, and mouth and had begun washing him down. Davey watched, speechless.

Once the baby was scrubbed and swaddled in blankets, they brought him over to Davey. He was wearing a hospital issued gown and a little blue knit cap that was also standard hospital issued. Davey held him, staring at his own features reflected in the face of his son, and felt the deepest connection he'd ever felt to anyone. He wanted to hold the boy forever and never let him go, to be the type of loving father he'd always wanted but never had. He knew that he had failed miserably so far. He'd been fired from his construction job in April, a week after Geraldo Rivera got his nose broken on TV by a group of skinheads. His boss insisted that it was just a lay-off, not a termination, and that there was no connection between the two events but the man's disgust had been obvious and unabashed. His name had been Theodore Neiderman. Davey was fairly certain that was a Jewish name. After he lost his job, things between him and Cindy had worsened. She'd been nice to him as long as he'd been bringing in money regularly, once the child support payments became erratic, her moods had done likewise.

"Don't start anything with me when you come, okay?" Cindy asked.

"Why would I start anything?"

"I mean, don't start all the interrogation shit and trying to get me to come back. I don't want to get another restraining order. We're through."

"We should have gotten married."

She sighed, even louder this time and Davey punched the phone booth again.

"Davey, you're a racist. I don't want Mickey being raised that way. I'm going to college. I'm going to make sure he has a good life. What can you do for him?"

Davey closed his eyes and bit his lip, trying hard not to think about what she was saying, not to let it affect him, but her words hurt and worse, they made him want to hurt her back.

"I'm his father, Cindy. I can give him that. I'll see you in an hour."

He hung up the phone and punched the metal booth until his knuckles bled. He was breathing hard and tears streamed down his face.

Why doesn't anyone understand me? Why are they all so fucking blind?

Little Davey left the WAWA food market, keeping an eye out for the cops. He needed to get some money now and mugging somebody was out of the question. If he got arrested, the cops would find the knife and pin that stabbing on him. Even if that faggot survived he'd get fifteen years minimum for attempted murder and assault with a deadly weapon. Besides, he wasn't some common criminal. Mugging people was for niggers, spics, and low-lifes. That left one alternative, borrowing the money from his dad.

Fuck. This is gonna be fun.

The last thing Little Davey wanted was to ask his father for anything. He would never admit it to himself, but deep down he hated the man. His father had never fully recovered after his mother left. He drank too much and was violent when he was intoxicated which was more often than not. Davey's only hope was to catch him when he first got home and was still on his first beer.

ELEVEN

5:45 pm

The trio of black teens eyed Skinner murderously as he passed them. He could smell marijuana and alcohol on their breath. He could feel their animosity. It was like passing through a dense cloud of hate. It made his eyes water.

Skinner kept his head down and looked straight ahead. He wished that he had a cap or a hoodie to hide his bald head. Instead, his pale scalp glowed like a celestial body. The three teenagers were drawn to him like the pull of gravity.

"Hey, you fuckin' skinhead! You wunna them damn Nazis ain't you?"

Skinner ducked his head as far down between his shoulders as he could and continued walking. He didn't turn to look at the speaker but sped up his stride. The three teens sped up to match his pace, surrounding him. One of them pushed him hard from behind, nearly sending him sprawling.

"I'm talkin' to you, white boy! You fuckin' ignorin' me? I heard about you racist skinhead motherfuckers on TV. Ya'll hate niggas, huh? Think you're fuckin' better than us?"

The short skinny kid who'd pushed him, took out a wad of hundred dollar bills and waved them in Skinner's face. "I could buy and sell your bitch ass, white boy. What the fuck have you got? I could pay a crackhead five dollars to smoke your punk-ass! That's how much you're worth, you fuckin' skinhead motherfucker!"

Fuckin', Geraldo Rivera. Ever since that damn show aired, everybody was out to get them.

He knew he would have to answer them eventually.

84

Either that or catch a beatdown for his silence. Skinner was beginning to tremble. He tried to walk faster but now they were all pushing and shoving him around. He raised his shoulders and ducked lower, expecting a punch any moment.

He cast a quick glance at the two guys on either side of him and the one behind. There were two small guys, one skinny and one fat, and one huge guy who was even bigger than Bo. He snickered, thinking that he'd run into the black version of their little crew.

"Fuck are you laughing about, skinhead?"

Skinner laughed harder. He found his balls finally and turned to give one of those jiggaboos a piece of his mind. He turned his head and found himself staring right down the barrel or a large, black, automatic pistol. Skinner looked around for a way of escape. Seeing none, he turned back to face the little guy with the gun.

"Fuck you, nigger. White Power!"

He saw the muzzle flash but never heard the gunshot. Never even felt it.

TWELVE

Amtrak, 6:59 pm

The train hadn't yet left the station when Mack spotted the five skinheads in the next car walking toward him. They were looking directly at him. One of them smiled, licked his lips, and began nodding his head. Another one pointed in Mack's direction then pounded his fist into the palm of his other hand. They obviously knew who he was and had come looking for him.

"Shit."

Mack wasn't completely unarmed. He had the two daggers in his belt buckle but he preferred blunt instruments, something he could use to pummel these fuckers into submission. He had nothing and they were almost there. The door to his car opened and the little gang of skinheads stepped in. There were more than a dozen other people in the car with him, but Mack held no illusions that any of them would rush to his defense. In Philadelphia, people tended to mind their business, which often meant ignoring the plight of the victimized. Mack stood up on his seat. If he was going to be outnumbered, he at least wanted the advantage of higher ground.

None of the skinheads was larger than six foot or weighed more than a hundred and eighty pounds. That made things slightly better, but not much. At least they weren't all big steroid freaks.

One of them asked.

"Are you Mack?"

Mack didn't answer. Didn't ask them what they wanted

to know for, if they were racist skinheads or SHARP, if they were looking for a fight, revenge, or wanted to congratulate him. He kicked the guy who asked in the jaw with his steel-toed motorcycle boot and smiled at the satisfying sound of teeth cracking and the guy's jaw unhinging. The skinhead crumpled to the floor, spitting teeth, with blood oozing from his mouth.

The next guy stepped into his place and Mack took a kick at him but missed. The skinhead ducked and then he and his buddies charged. Mack had to squat down to avoid being tackled. He swung a hook at one of his attackers that caught the guy high on the temple which wobbled him but didn't take him off his feet. He launched a straight right at another one that shattered the guy's nose and sent him reeling backwards. Mack took a punch to the side of the head that felt like he'd been hit with a pillow but when he turned to look for his assailant he was struck from the other side with a blow that felt like a baseball bat. Flashbulbs went off in his head. His eyesight blurred and he went down as more punches fell. The back of Mack's head struck the train wall, just below the window and he could feel his head slam against the wall repeatedly as someone punched him.

Mack could taste his own blood. He knew he was being kicked and punched but could no longer feel the blows. There was a crushing weight on his chest that he recognized as the weight of a body, someone was straddling his chest while they punched him in the face. He was losing consciousness and if that happened, he'd probably never wake up. Mack groped for his belt buckle and slid out the daggers. Without thinking, he slashed and jabbed at the bodies pressed tight against him. Blood began to flow. Shouts and cries of pain echoed in his head, sounding like they were coming from underwater. Mack still couldn't see what was going on. His eyesight hadn't cleared and his vision darkened, blurred, and everything began to spin, which made him want to throw up. He stabbed upward with the knife and felt it sink into something soft then felt a warm rush of blood pour out over his hands. It bled like a mortal wound.

Abruptly, all the weight was gone.

Mack sat up and slashed with the daggers, one clutched in each hand.

"They're gone. You're okay," said a male voice from Mack's left. The voice had a practiced tone of bored indifference. The kind you picked up on the streets, where violence was an everyday occurrence and looking or sounding too interested in someone else's plight could quickly add your name to the victim's pool.

Mack blinked several times and wiped his eyes with the back of his fists, leaving smears of blood on his forehead and cheeks. His eyesight cleared and he could see the guy with the lackadaisical voice, sitting a few seats behind him. He was a large black man in his mid-thirties with a shaved head and prison tattoos on his neck. His indifference toward violence was likely no mere affectation.

The skinheads who'd attacked Mack were retreating into the next car, bruised and bleeding, dragging the guy he'd kicked in the face and another guy with a black moustache and a five-o'clock shadow of black hair dusting his shaved scalp. The guy with the moustache was bleeding from the stomach and screaming about not wanting to die while he held his guts in with both hands.

I need to get the fuck out of here, Mack thought, looking around for an exit. It didn't matter that they'd attacked him. He was black and they were white and he'd been carrying illegal weapons and may have killed one of them. If the cops came, Mack was certain that he would not get the benefit of the doubt. There was also the possibility that the three uninjured skinheads would regroup and attack again. That possibility was slim but it couldn't be ignored. Either way, staying on the train was a dumb idea. Mack looked out the window. It was too dark to tell what station they were near. He could only hope that wherever he got off the train wasn't too far from a bus or a subway or too deep within North Philly. In his neighborhood, everyone knew Mack and nobody tripped on how he dressed. But a tall skinny black guy with short dreadlocks shaved into a Mohawk, wearing a leather motorcycle jacket, motorcycle boots, big silver hoop earrings, and spiked wristbands would be an irresistible target in the drug-ravaged, war-torn streets of North Philly. It didn't matter that he was black too. He didn't live there and he dressed funny. In North Philly after dark, he would be just as much of an outsider as a white guy in a business suit and just about as safe.

Fuck it. I ain't got much choice, Mack thought. The train screeched and squealed into the empty station, pausing just long enough for Mack to hop off before rocketing off again. The skinheads glared at Mack through the train window as it pulled out of the station. He knew he would be seeing them again, and next time there would be more of them. Jason was right about that. These guys had come hunting for him. They knew his name and they had come looking for him. Next time, they might even come armed, especially now that they knew he was.

Mack looked around the graffiti-covered station. He had no idea where he was. The sign had been torn down and the streets looked unfamiliar. There was a bus stop nearby and Mack turned his collar up against the wind and walked toward it. If he knew what bus stop he was at it would go a long way to telling him where he was. He was halfway across the street when he heard several voices call out from the direction he'd just come from.

"Where the fuck you from? You tryin'a look like Rick James or somebody? You supposed to be the king of punk funk or some shit?"

At first, Mack thought that it was the skinheads, coming

to try their luck again, but the inflections, the tone, the slang, was all wrong. Those were North Philly accents. Black urban accents.

Fuck.

If there was anything Mack hated about this city it was the omnipresent threat of violence. Only in Philly could you be fighting skinheads one minute and niggas the next. Mack laughed at the irony. He felt like he was in that old 70's movie *The Warriors*. Any minute now he expected to hear a shaky high-pitched voice calling, "*Waaaaarrioooors, come out and plaaaaayyyy!*"

"Fuck you laughin' at, Rick James?" This voice was deeper, huskier than the first and was followed by the unmistakable click and ching of an automatic pistol being cocked and a round chambered. Shit had just gotten serious. Mack looked in back of him, in the direction of the sound and saw several large anthropoid shapes headed toward him. Mack was smart enough, this time, not to try to be a hero. He took off running at a full sprint. He heard a gunshot but didn't feel anything strike him. There was loud laughter behind him.

"You'd better run, you little bitch!"

He kept running.

THIRTEEN

Davey's house, 7:36 pm

An old BMX bike sat rusting on the lawn. Davey remembered how hard he had to work to get that bike. His father made him mow the lawn and rake the leaves every Saturday for a month. He had to wash the dishes every night, do the laundry, and clean the garage. That weekend he had to paint the house alone. He had never painted anything before and Big Dave yelled and cursed at him the entire time. Little Davey cried several times and received a slap for it more than once, but finally, he got the job done. Then his father had gotten drunk and fell asleep and little Davey had to beg him for the money he was owed. His dad finally snapped out of his drunken stupor long enough to slap Little Davey upside the head for waking him up, but Davey was persistent. Finally, his father relented and gave him the money but he was too drunk to drive. Little Davey rode a bus to Toys r' Us and picked out his bike. It took him two hours to ride his new bike all the way home. He was exhausted when he finally staggered into the house, but he couldn't remember ever being so happy. He was eleven years old then and, until his son was born, he'd never been that happy again.

The house was still painted pale blue with white trim, the same color Davey had painted it nine years ago. The paint on the wood siding had begun to flake and chip. Davey hadn't asked his father for anything since the day he'd bought him the bike so he hadn't been forced to paint the house since. That was likely to change if he walked in and asked him for money to buy his kid diapers. Little Davey took a deep breath and walked up the stairs, already pissed off, imagining his father's condescending reply.

The house smelled of dirty laundry, stale beer, rotting fast food, urine, and more beer. The TV was on, creating a strobe light effect in the dark room as it flickered with the image of Peggy Bundy berating her wisecracking husband. The place looked like a frat house. A pile of empty pizza boxes sat on the coffee table, nearly three feet high. Beside it sat several cardboard buckets filled with chicken bones. The floor was littered with empty beer cans and liquor bottles. Little Davey shook his head in disgust. He'd stopped cleaning out of protest, hoping that his dad would get up off his drunken lazy ass and start throwing away his own garbage and washing his own dishes, but apparently the old man was content to live in filth.

Davey's dad sat in his lounge chair with a bottle of MD 20/20 on his lap. He was in his pajamas, the same ones he'd been wearing all week. He was awake… barely. He stared at the screen for a long moment as if he was confused by what he was seeing. Then his eyes began to close and his head dropped forward. Little Davey had to resist the urge to punch the man right in the mouth.

What a fucking waste. Davey wondered, not for the first time, if they really were any better than niggers, spics, and Jews.

"Dad. Wake up. This place looks like shit! How the fuck can you live like this?"

Big Dave lifted his head, opened his eyes, and immediately took a deep swig of MD before turning to look at his son.

"If you'd clean this shithole like you're supposed to, it wouldn't look this way."

Davey bristled.

"I'm not your fuckin' maid!"

Big Dave took another swig of MD then turned back to

the TV. Christina Applegate was prancing across the screen in tight pink stretch pants and a white halter top that made her tits look exceptionally perky. You could almost see the outline of her nipples through the fabric.

"Well, what fuckin' good are you then?"

Again, Little Davey had to resist the urge to hit the old man.

"I need money. Mickey needs diapers."

Big Dave shrugged.

"How the fuck is that my problem?"

"He's your grandson!"

Big Dave took another swig, emptying the bottle of Mad Dog. He turned and looked longingly toward the kitchen. Little Davey smiled.

"You want me to get you a beer, old man?"

Big Dave frowned and tried to stand up, almost pitching himself out of the recliner onto his face. He leaned over and steadied himself with one hand on the coffee table, knocking over an ashtray that was overloaded with ashes and cigarette butts.

"I'll get it myself."

"Or die trying," Little Davey added.

Big Dave gave him the finger in lieu of a verbal response.

"Look, this place is a fucking mess. You give me thirty dollars and I'll clean it up for you and go shopping for you so you have some food in that refrigerator. I'll even buy you more beer."

Big Dave was still bent over, wobbling, trying to keep from falling on his ass. He crawled back into the recliner.

"Why don't you start by getting me another fucking beer? My wallet's on the dresser. I just cashed my check yesterday. Don't take none of it. I'll give you what I want to give you. Just bring it to me."

Just cashed your welfare check, you mean, Little Davey thought, sneering as if he'd just tasted something particularly foul. He knew that his dad hadn't gotten much work lately and had secretly snuck off to the welfare office to apply for assistance. It was against everything Little Davey had been taught to believe, everything his dad had taught him to believe, and it sickened him.

"Oh, and I need to borrow your gun too."

Big Dave raised an eyebrow.

"Should I ask?"

"No."

.

FOURTEEN

Jason's house, 7:55 pm

Jason sat in his bedroom, listening to a local hardcore band called *The Meat Sword* and trying his best not to hear his parents argue about him.

"Why'd you say he could stay here tonight? Just when we were starting to put our life back together. He doesn't care about us! He doesn't care about anyone! All he does is destroy things and now he's destroying us! Again!"

"Shhhh. He'll hear you."

"Of course he will. That little sneak is always listening!"

Jason turned up the volume and sang at the top of his lungs.

"... I'm a monster
a stone cold killer
I'm a monster
A stone cold killer
You should watch yourself
You might get hurt
Like you hurt me
You might get hurt
Like you hurt me..."

Jason fingered a buck knife he'd stolen from a record store on Market Street. The blade wasn't very sharp, but he was confident that it would do the job if he ever needed it to. He wished that Mack wasn't such a mamma's boy. Jason knew that he could never kill anyone himself, but with Mack around, he felt fucking invincible. If he thought for a second that he could talk Mack into killing his parents with him,

95

he'd have made those fuckers suffer. A tear ran down his cheek as Jason stabbed his mattress with the knife.

Why don't they love me? Why do they always want to get rid of me?

But Jason already knew the answer to that. He hated to be told what to do, especially by men and his step-dad least of all. That had created immediate friction between them. His step-father had tried to solve the issue with frequent beatings, thinking that it would whip Jason in line but it had made him even more rebellious. He felt like the man had taken his mother away from him and she had been perfectly complicit in the whole thing. She always took his side on everything. She didn't notice how Jason's grades had begun to slip immediately after she married that asshole. She didn't notice how Jason had begun to drink and smoke and listen to hardcore music. She didn't notice how he'd begun dying his hair black and wearing black eyeliner and leather jackets and spikes. She didn't notice anything that Jason did. He doubted she'd even noticed when he'd stopped coming home.

Padre had told him to confront her about it, tell her how he felt, but that would mean admitting that he felt anything which he wasn't quite ready to do. He plugged in his headphones and slipped them over his ears. It was a compromise. Now, they wouldn't have to hear his music but he still wouldn't have to hear them.

He wanted to go out, talk to Padre again, maybe even get drunk, but he was afraid that his parents wouldn't let him back in if he did. Besides, the streets weren't safe for him without Mack. Those skinheads were all just looking for the chance to catch the two of them apart and Jason had no illusions about his chances of surviving an attack by even two or three skinheads without Mack by his side. As Mack always said, he was "knee-high to a grasshopper". As much as he loved to fight, when it came down to it, he was just a little guy. He'd get squashed like a bug if he got attacked by himself. So that meant spending the night in the house, alone, listening to his parents bitch and complain.

Man, this fucking sucks, Jason thought. He couldn't wait until tomorrow night when Mack came back. He had an idea that they should go see Miranda before the concert. That might give Mack the fuel he needed to do some real damage to those Nazi bastards.

I can't wait, Jason thought. *This is going to be fucking epic!*

FIFTEEN

Germantown, 9:01pm

The bus ride back to Germantown had taken over an hour.
Mack staggered off the bus, barely awake. He was exhausted.
He hurt all over as a result of the beating he'd taken from the
skinheads and he was terrified that the police would be waiting
for him when he arrived home and that he'd be arrested for
aggravated assault, assault with a deadly weapon, and maybe
even attempted homicide. Unless, of course, the kid didn't
make it, then he'd be fighting murder or manslaughter charges.
He thought back to the body he and Jason had dropped off in
the lot earlier. His chest felt heavy. If they found Billy's body,
he might be facing murder charges anyway.

Mack walked up the hill to his house, wondering if anyone
had seen the Suzuki, and trying to console himself by telling
himself that there were hundreds of white Suzuki Samurais
on the road and that nobody ever noticed license plates. He
knew that he was going to have to avoid those Jersey girls for
a while. If someone had spotted the vehicle and it was known
that he and Jason regularly hung out with girls who drove a
Suzuki, it wouldn't take the police long to put two and two
together.

I am so fucked.

The neighborhood was quiet. The streets were unusually
empty for so early in the evening, but it was cold out and
there was still snow on the ground. Cold weather tended to
drive even the hardest hoodrats in doors.

The houses looked somehow cleaner covered in white
snow, less depressed. The trees looked beautiful, like a

98

winter wonderland. The air even smelled cleaner, crisper. The night sky was so clear that you could see every star in the heaven. Mack was staring up at the sky when someone in a big hooded ski jacket with fur around the collar stepped out from behind a large shrub and pointed a gun in his face. He'd been caught slippin' and now he was a dead man.

I love you, Mom. And I love you too, Miranda.

Mack stared hard at the gunman. He wanted to remember the guy's face on the off-chance that there was an afterlife and he would get the chance to see the bastard again. He wanted to remember him, so that he could pay him back in the next life. The guy was fat, pudgy and his skin was pockmarked. He looked familiar.

"Give me your money or I'll blow your fuckin' head off."

A robbery. That's better. A little better. At least the guy isn't tryin' to kill me. He just wants money.

Then Mack placed the face. He knew the guy. They'd gone to elementary school together. He knew the guy's mom and his two brothers. They lived two blocks away.

"Sid? It's me! Mack."

The gun didn't waver. There was no recognition in the guy's eyes. His eyes were glassy, the pupils dilated as wide as the gun barrel. He was high as fuck.

"Sid! It's me, man. It's Mack! Get that fuckin' gun out my face."

Still no recognition.

"Give me your fuckin' money! I ain't playin'!"

He cocked the gun.

"I ain't playin' either! Get that fuckin' gun out my face, Sid!"

Slowly, recognition seeped back into Sid's eyes.

"Awww, man. I was just playin' with you! You should have seen your face! Why you all beat up like that? Somebody kick your ass?" Sid laughed. But Mack had seen his eyes. Sid hadn't been playin'. He was so high that he hadn't recognized Mack. He'd known him since he was ten-years-old and he had been ready to put a bullet in Mack's brain.

"Yeah, funny." Mack walked past him, shaking his head.

"I was just playin' wit you, man! Why you trippin'?"

Mack didn't look back. If Sid wanted to get mad about it, he could shoot him in the back, but Mack was tired, sore, and not in the mood. This was the third time tonight that someone had threatened his life. It wasn't a completely atypical day in Philly. Philadelphia wasn't the murder capital but it was in the top ten. Fights and gunshots were common everyday occurrences and that adrenaline dump that came with the "fight or flight" instinct was something that Mack felt five or six times a day on average. Still, this damn sure wasn't one of his better days.

He wanted to kill Sid. The only thing preventing him was the soreness in his muscles and the gun in Sid's hand. He walked the remaining blocks to his house, feeling like he could collapse at any moment.

Mack knew that the violence that surrounded him was not just a problem with Philly. It was a problem with him. It was a direct result of who and what he was, what he had willingly become. Philadelphia was definitely a tough town. No question there. But his lifestyle was making it tougher. Where he lived, how he dressed, the friends he chose, the places he hung out, even the music he listened to, were all magnets for violence. It was only a matter of time before that violence overcame him. But, at least on this day, he had once again prevailed over it, once again survived. Still, it felt like his time and his luck were beginning to run out.

He turned the corner onto Ambrose Street and felt an immediate wave of relief flood over him. He was alive. He hadn't been shot. There were no police parked outside his house and his mom's car was there. She was home. The light was on in the living room and he could hear the television.

She was awake. He walked up to the door and rang the doorbell.

His mom was in her house robe with curlers in her hair when she opened the door.

"Hi, Mom."

She reached out to touch his swollen face.

"What the hell happened to you?"

"I was just playin' with some friends. We got a little rough. No biggie."

Her eyes narrowed as she looked at him closer.

"You weren't out there fightin' again were you? I told you, you ain't a kid no more. You're nineteen now. They'll take you to jail for fighting!"

"I know, Mom. Don't worry. I'm not going to jail."

Not yet anyway.

"Were you doing that slam dancing?"

Mack smiled. His mother had been trying her best lately to understand his new lifestyle. He loved her for that.

"Yeah, sort of."

"That just don't make no sense to me. Out there hurtin' yourselves for fun. I think you should call that college back and see if you can get in there right now. The streets ain't no good for you. You know your friend Lamar got shot the other day, up there on the avenue. I heard he was messin' around with drugs or somethin'."

Mack shrugged.

"He wasn't really a friend. He was older than me. He used to beat me up all the time when I was little. Lamar was kind of a jerk. Once I grew up, he would run from me like a little punk."

"Oh, don't talk that way about dead people. It ain't nice."

"I'm sorry, Mom."

"Now, come on over here and give your momma a hug and a kiss. It feels like I ain't seen you in days. What's out in them streets that's so exciting it keeps you out all night?

Ain't nothin' in this town open after two am but legs."

"Well, that's enough to keep me out all night."

Mack smiled and winked.

"Oh, you're terrible. You're just like your granddaddy. You know, Pop was a real ladies man when he was young. You got that honest. It's in your blood."

Mack leaned down and kissed his mother on the cheek, hugging her tight. Whenever she talked about him inheriting any male characteristics it was always from his grandfather or great grandfather. She never mentioned his father at all. Mack had never met his dad and never wanted to. He knew the man lived in the neighborhood somewhere or had at one time, but Mack had never seen him or if he had, he never knew who it was. His mother had gone to great pains to keep "that bad influence" away from him and he had respected her wishes. If she said that he was better off not knowing him then Mack believed her. His mother had been all the parent he'd ever needed.

Mack's mother was a tall woman with strong angular facial features, high cheek bones, a strong jaw, and dark piercing eyes that she attributed to "Indian blood" like half the black people Mack knew. It was like black folks couldn't stand the idea of being completely black. They had to validate themselves by adding something else to their racial composition as if black wasn't good enough. But the truth was that Mack's great-grandmother had been Seminole. He just didn't talk about it because he didn't want to sound like the rest of the self-haters. As far as he was concerned, his family was black. That was enough.

"Hey, where's Jonas?"

Jonas was his mother's boyfriend, a big, corn-fed country white boy almost as tall as Mack and twice as heavy. He looked like a reject from Mayberry. Mack used to work for Jonas at his construction company. That's how his mom met the guy. The two of them made the most unusual couple imaginable but he made his mother happy… usually,

"He kept looking in my pots while I was cooking. You know I hate when people look in my pots when I'm cooking, gettin' all in my way. So, I kicked him out."

"You kicked him out? Of the house?"

"Yeah!"

"So, when's he's coming back?"

"He ain't coming back. I kicked him out I tole' you."

Mack couldn't believe what he was hearing.

"You mean for good?"

She nodded.

"I told him to pack up all his shit and get the hell outta my house. Yes, I did."

"Mom…"

He wanted to tell his mother that she had to learn to give a little, that she needed to be able to compromise and overlook some things, but he knew it wouldn't have done any good. She had been single too long, ever since his father left them. She had been used to ruling the household. Compromise wasn't in her vocabulary.

"… are you guys off for good then?"

"Off? We ain't off. We're still dating. I just can't live with him. He'll be here tomorrow."

Mack smiled and shook his head.

"I'm gonna go upstairs and take a nap then work out for a while."

"You hungry? I know you ain't been eatin' right. You look so skinny. I've got some fried chicken in the refrigerator from last night. I can heat it up for you? "

Mack smiled.

"You don't have to do that. I like it cold. I'll just throw some hot sauce on it. You go ahead and get some rest. How was work today?"

"Oh, you know how it is. Them white folks tryin'a run your poor mother into the ground."

Mack smiled. With the exception of the skinheads, Mack had never really experienced real racism. His mother's own prejudices struck him as quaint and a bit of an odd contradiction considering Jonas. In her mind, white people were still conspiring to keep black people down. She considered it a mere matter of time before the white girls that Mack sometimes brought home called him a nigger in a fit of rage. Strange, she never thought of Jonas that way. To her, he was always an exception though Mack thought it far more likely that nigger would slip out of Jonas' mouth than from any of the girls he dated. The man had a tendency to defend the wrong things, like racial profiling and doing away with Affirmative Action programs. His mother defended him by saying he was just from a different era. *Like the Klan is from a different era?* Mack thought. But he never said it. He didn't hate the guy. Jonas was actually a pretty nice guy. He was good to his mother, generous and loving. There was just something off about him. Mack had once gone through the man's video tape collection and found a tape that contained nothing but black porn and episodes of "Soul Train". The man had a fetish and Mack was sure that his fetish was the only reason he was with his mom. It was more than a little disgusting. But his mom was blind to it and she was happy and whatever made his mom happy was cool with Mack.

Despite her relationship with Jonas, Mack's mother still held onto her own militant stance on most racial issues. She had been a black panther in the early seventies and Mack could remember going on marches with her. Though he never directly said so, he knew that she was still waiting for "The Revolution". She expected a racial civil war to erupt at any minute. In her way, she was just as ignorant in regards to race as the skinheads. But, in her way, she was also right. A racial civil war was about to happen and it would probably happen on South Street with Mack right in the center of it. Only it wouldn't be as clear cut as blacks against whites. It would be racist assholes with shaved heads against guys in leather and spikes with Mohawks and Technicolor hairdos.

Mack leaned in and kissed his mother on the forehead. "Good night, Mom. I'll see you in the morning."

SIXTEEN

Cindy's house, 9:34 pm

"It's too late. He's asleep and I'm not waking him up. You should have come earlier."

Little Davey rolled his eyes and grit his teeth. Cindy got on his nerves more than any other human being on earth. Just the tone of her voice could throw him into a violent rage. Holding in his temper now was taking a Herculean effort, but flipping out would only result in him going to jail where they might even link him to the stabbing of the queer in the Michael Jackson get-up. At the least, she'd get a restraining order and he'd never see his kid again.

"I'm sorry. I had to go grocery shopping for my dad when I went to pick up the diapers."

Cindy put one hand on her hip and twisted her pursed lips sideways on her face. She looked at him like he was a bug on a windshield.

"You could have just given me the money. I would have picked up his diapers."

"I brought you some money too, but I ain't given you shit if I can't see my kid."

For a brief moment it looked like she was going to challenge him but then she relented and opened the door to let him in.

"He's upstairs. I'll go get him. You stay down here. You can't stay long though. My boyfriend is coming over. It wouldn't be cool for you to be here when he gets here."

"Who the fuck is this boyfriend and why are you letting this dude around my kid?"

Cindy was a small girl, just over five feet tall and barely over a hundred pounds but she had the attitude of a five-hundred pound gorilla. She didn't back down from anyone and that had made for a bad match. They always butted heads and it usually ended with her throwing something at him, him hitting her, her hitting back, and the cops intervening. When they were still together, weekends usually ended with one of them in jail.

"Who he is, is none of your fuckin' business and I'll let whoever the hell I want into *MY* house! If you want to start paying my bills then you can start having a say in what goes on here. Otherwise, mind your own damn business!"

"My son *IS* my business! Who is he?"

"He's my boyfriend! What else do you need to know?"

"Is he black?"

Cindy's mouth dropped open.

"What did you just say?"

"Your boyfriend, is he a fucking nigger?"

"Get out of my house."

"I'm not going anywhere until I see my son."

Cindy stepped up until she was nose to nose with Davey then screamed at the top of her lungs pointing at the front door.

"GET THE HELL OUT OF MY HOUSE!!!"

Davey cupped her entire face in his hand and pushed her back. He turned and headed for the door. She punched him in the back of his head and he turned and palmed her face again, pushing her down on her ass. Then he opened the front door.

"Get the fuck out, you fucking loser!"

"I'm coming back to see my son tomorrow and if there's any guys here when I get here you're both going to regret it."

Cindy scrambled back to her feet.

"Are you threatening me? Get out of my house you little-dick piece of shit!"

The muscles in Davey's jaw hurt from biting down. His

body began to tremble with adrenalin-fueled rage.

"I will kill you, you fucking cunt. If you don't let me see my son, I will fucking kill you."

There was no bravado in his voice. He didn't even yell. It was stated as a simple fact. He turned and walked out of the house, slamming the door behind him.

SEVENTEEN

Bo's apartment, 10:15 pm.

"Why do you hang out with those losers? Aren't you getting a little old for all of this skinhead shit?" Gia asked. She was cuddled up next to Bo on the bed with her head resting on his chest and his seed drying on her belly. Bo had been just about to drift off to sleep. He wiped away a line of drool that had dribbled out the corner of his mouth and blinked himself awake.

"W-what?"

"Skinner and Little Davey? Why the hell do you hang out with those idiots? You know they're only going to get you into trouble. They're kind of crazy. You know, I heard that Skinner used to torture animals when he was a kid and Little Davey just takes this whole Nazi thing way too far. Why would you hang out with guys like that?"

Bo shrugged. "It's what I believe and don't tell me you like Jews and niggers any more than I do. I've met your family. Your dad is the most racist sonuvabitch I know."

"You should see how he talks about *you* behind your back. He calls you my "pct paddy" or "that big Irish Leprechaun". He doesn't like anyone who isn't Italian. Except he doesn't go around shaving his head and joining a club."

"Why are you bringing this shit up? You knew what I was about when you met me."

Gia looked at him with obvious worry in her eyes.

"What is it?"

"I was watching the news today. They found a body in the projects in Philly, near South Street where you guys hang

109

out. It was a skinhead. Somebody bashed his brains out."

"It wasn't one of us was it?"

"I don't know. I didn't recognize the name. They think he got killed trying to buy drugs down there. His family said he had a drug problem but they said he wasn't a skinhead like you guys. They said he was against racism."

"But they killed him anyway. See, it doesn't matter how you treat these animals."

Gia hugged him closer, nuzzling his beard.

"I just don't want anything to happen to you. I love you."

"I love you too, Gia and don't worry. Ain't nothing gonna happen to me."

The phone rang and Bo and Gia looked at each other. Immediately, they both knew it wasn't good news. Good news seldom came after 10pm. Bo crawled from the covers, disengaging Gia's embrace and slipping out from beneath her head. As he walked to the phone, he was expecting it to be Little Davey or Skinner calling from the police station to tell him they were all going down for murder. He was surprised when he picked up the phone and heard Skinner's mom on the other end.

"Bo?" the voice was shaky, cracking with emotion.

"Mrs. McDowell?"

"Evan's dead. They killed my boy!"

"Evan? Skinner? What happened? Who killed him?"

Bo wondered if it had been his body the police found in Philly but Gia said she'd seen it on the news this morning and Skinner had been with them until a few hours ago. It couldn't have been him. Maybe his mother had gotten it wrong. Skinner couldn't be dead.

"His name was Evan! Call him by his name!"

"Sorry. Sorry, Mrs. McDowell. What happened to Evan?"

There was a long pause and Bo could hear the faint sounds of weeping from the other end of the phone.

"He was walking home and he got jumped by a bunch

of black guys. They shot him in the head! Those fucking niggers killed my baby! I'm sorry. I shouldn't have said that. God, please forgive me."

Bo took a long deep breath.

"Don't worry, Mrs. McDowell. We'll pay them back. We won't let Evan die in vain."

"No! It was your fault! You and that other little degenerate you hang out with. You killed him! They shot him because of the way he was dressed. Because of all this skinhead nonsense. They said he was a racist, a Nazi. That's what killed him! You just stay away from me and my family. I don't want you anywhere near us. I just wanted you to know what you did!"

"I'm sor—"

The phone clicked and the dial tone wined in his ear. Bo hung up, shaken, afraid of what would happen when Little Davey and the rest of *The Unrest* found out what happened. Maybe Gia was right. Maybe it *was* time to get out.

EIGHTEEN

A woman with tight, shiny, white skin from too many plastic surgeries and blonde hair squeezed into a puritanical bun, sat at her desk in the Channel 11 newsroom. On a large screen behind her, the Martin Luther King projects loomed. A coroner's van was parked amid several police cruisers. A small crowd of African Americans had gathered. They seemed to be celebrating, smiling and laughing into the camera. Two men in dark blue jumpsuits with "Medical Examiner" stenciled on the back carried a gurney with a long black vinyl bag on it that presumably contained a body. And Mack knew exactly whose body it was.

Shit!

The camera panned over to the empty lot with the piles of trash and broken furniture. Mack turned up the sound.

"*... the victim is believed to be affiliated with a skinhead group. Police speculate that he may have come to the Martin Luther King projects for the purpose of purchasing drugs. The victim's shaved head, leather jacket, and combat boots, usually associated with Nazi separatist groups, may have instigated the assault. Skinheads and other Nazi groups have achieved recent notoriety following an on-air brawl on the Geraldo Rivera show. Police have no suspects at this time. Drug-related crimes have been on the rise in Philadelphia...*"

Mack's eyes glazed over as he listened to the newswoman drone on. Soon, he couldn't hear her at all. He was trying to decide if this meant they had gotten away with it or if the cops were just withholding information, trying to make the real killers believe that they weren't suspects while they gathered more evidence and prepared to make their arrest.

112

If they thought it was drug-related and were blaming the hoodrats in the projects for it then that meant that he and Jason were clear. But there was no way to be sure. Only time would tell. The camera shifted to the living room of an older couple. They were Billy's parents.

"... he wasn't a racist. He used to date a black girl. He grew up in a mixed neighborhood. He had a drug problem but he wasn't a Nazi. Why did they have to kill him?"

Mack felt like shit.

There was a noise behind him and all the hairs stood up on the back of his neck. Mack leapt from the couch and spun around with his fists raised.

"What are you so jumpy for? You look like you've seen a ghost."

Mack stared at his mother. His heart was racing. He lowered his fists, still breathing heavily.

"What the matter, baby? Why are you so worked up? Did I scare you?"

Mack fumbled for the right words, trying to decide whether he should confide in her or not. He looked down at the TV, but they had moved on to some celebrity-worship drivel about Madonna wannabes. When he looked back at his mother, his bottom lip was trembling and there were tears in his eyes.

"Ohhh, baby. What's wrong?" She rushed over and wrapped her arms around him which unleashed the floodgates. He began to sob openly.

"What's wrong, baby? Tell me what's the matter? Whatever it is, we can work through it. You know your momma will fix it."

Mack sniffled a few times as he wiped away his tears.

"Not this time, momma. You can't help me with this."

"What is it?"

The concern in her eyes was so genuine, so profound, that Mack had to struggle to hold back another outbreak of tears. Disappointing his mother was the worst thing he could imagine. But he was afraid that if he told her, she'd want him to go to the police. He thought about it a moment longer before he decided.

"I think I may have accidentally killed someone."

It hung there in the room like a dank cloud between them. The silence was stifling and oppressive. Mack didn't breathe until she spoke.

"Do the police know?"

Mack shook his head. His mother nodded, looking up at the ceiling in deep thought.

"Is there anything to connect you to it? Did you leave any evidence?"

Mack shrugged.

"I don't know. I don't think so."

She sighed heavily and shook her head.

"Well, tell me how it happened."

Mack told her about Billy getting high and slamming his head against the walls and how they'd tried to throw him out of the house but he'd started yelling and throwing bottles. He told them about how Billy hit his head on the cement floor when Jason pushed him down the basement steps and finally how they'd used the Jersey girl's Suzuki to dump the body in the projects.

"Did anyone see the car?"

"They didn't say anything about it on the news."

She nodded, scratching her chin before rubbing an imaginary line of sweat from her brow.

"And you wouldn't want to turn your friend Jason in I assume?"

"No, I couldn't do that. It's just as much my fault and I helped hide the body."

"And you don't think he'd try to turn you in? He wouldn't make a deal with the police to save his own ass?"

This was not the line of questions Mack had been

expecting from his mother. She was calmer, more rational, than he ever would have imagined. It was almost spooky.

Mack shook his head slowly.

"No. He wouldn't do that. He's not like that."

She sighed again.

"Then you need to call that college back right now and get there as soon as possible. You need to get off the streets until this blows over. You can't stay here in Philly anymore."

NINETEEN

Jason's house, 9:17 am

"I'm leaving for work. Why don't you look for a job and clean up your room a little bit as long as you're here."

Jason was only half awake and in no mood for his stepfather's shit. He looked up to see the man standing in his doorway in a suit and tie with a briefcase in his hand. Jason's mother stood beyond him in the hallway looking nervous and fidgety.

Oh, here it comes. They're kicking me out again. Why does that dickless bastard always have to fuck with me?

"Don't worry. I'll be gone by the time you get back," Jason said.

"You don't have to leave. We're not kicking you out."

Sure you are.

"I'm just saying that if you're going to stay here you're going to have to find a job and help your mother out around here."

"I'm not staying. Like I said, it was just for the night. I'll be leaving in a few. Do you mind if I take a shower and get some breakfast first?"

Finally, Jason's mother stepped forward into the room, squeezing past her husband who looked amused despite the serious tone of his voice. He was getting off on this, delighting in Jason's discomfort. He held all the power and he knew it.

"Jason, of course you can take a shower. We're not kicking you out. You can stay as long as you like."

Jason snorted and chuckled.

116

"Yeah, right. You know how that will end. I think it's best for all of us if I get out of here."

Jason stood up and walked to his bedroom door. He grabbed the doorknob and slowly closed the door. His stepfather's hand was still holding the doorknob on the other side and a brief tug-of–war began.

"Do you mind? I need to get changed for a shower."

"Okay. Okay, sport. I'll see you around then."

His stepfather stared him in his eyes, challenging him, with a subtle smirk curling up one corner of his mouth. Jason returned the smirk and slowly closed the door. This time his stepfather did not resist.

Asshole.

Jason listened for the slam of the front door and the sound of his stepfather's car revving up for an annoyingly long time before driving off down the road. His stepfather drove a red Camaro that Jason called his "midlife crisis mobile". Jason hated that car almost as much as he hated his stepfather. It was another symbol of the man's enormous ego. Jason fantasized about destroying that vehicle with the same frequency that he fantasized about destroying the man himself. Jason could feel all the tension leave his body once he was certain the man was gone. He stripped out of his clothes, leaving them in a pile on the floor as he walked across the hall to the bathroom. If his mom saw him wandering the halls naked, so be it. She needed a shock or two to wake her up from her catatonia. Seeing her son's mature cock swinging from thigh to thigh might be just the thing to jar her to her senses. He laughed at the thought of it.

I'm sure I'm hung better than that asshole she's married to.

Jason stepped into the shower and felt almost instant relief as the warm spray took away the rest of his tension. He could feel the knotted chords in his neck and shoulders unwinding. He turned the spray novel on the showerhead to "pulsate" then turned the water temperature up higher until it was almost scalding, just below the limits of his pain tolerance. The anxiety and fear caused by Billy's death left him for a moment as he closed his eyes and luxuriated in the feel of the near boiling water firing into his upper back. He wanted to crawl back into bed and sleep for another couple of hours but didn't want to deal with his mother's complaints. If she tried to make him clean his room or take out the garbage it wouldn't end well.

In less than an hour, Jason had washed, changed clothes, stolen six dollars from his mother's purse, ate breakfast, and left. He walked up Ninth Street at a brisk pace, eager to get back to South Street where he could erase the stain of middle-class mediocrity from his mind. He refused to turn out like his parents. If the choice was between being beaten to death by skinheads or being an uptight, passionless, wage-slave, getting a nine-to-five, a BMW, voting Republican, and going to church on Sundays, he knew what his choice would be.

Despite his bravado, the idea of being cornered by a group of Nazi assholes without Mack beside him, terrified him. Once he made it to South Street, he knew he'd be okay. Even at ten o'clock in the morning there'd be a few punks there he knew. Some of his friends, like Chris and Breezy, worked on South Street. If it came down to it, they'd jump in before they'd let him get murdered. But it was unlikely that there would be any skinheads out until night. Most of them had jobs or were still in school. If this had been a weekend, he would not have been so bold.

Jason made it to South Street without incident. It was no wonder. The street was empty. The cold weather had reduced it to a graveyard. Even the usual crowd of shoppers from the mainline and sight-seeing history buffs who came to gawk at the Liberty Bell and Betsy Ross's house were staying away, delaying their foray into the city until the temperature rose.

He walked down to the hamburger shop where Breezy worked and was happy to find that she was there. Her long blonde hair was now in dreadlocks. She wore a frilly white vintage dress under her leather jacket and combat boots that came up to her knees with soles that were almost four inches thick. She'd obviously been shopping at *Trash & Vaudeville*.

"Hey Breezy! Cool hair. That looks badass!"

She smiled and clasped her hands in her lap, hunching her shoulders and turning slightly away, trying to look bashful.

"Thank you. I just wanted to do something different. You don't see a lot of white chicks with dreads."

"It looks awesome. Really. It looks great."

"Where's Mack?"

She looked behind him as if his five-foot-eight inch frame might have somehow been concealing the six-foot-six teenager.

"He went home to see his mom. You know Mack. He's always been a momma's boy and proud of it."

Breezy laughed.

"I didn't know that. That's funny. Kinda cute actually. He acts like such a jerk sometimes, always talking about how big his dick is and who he wants to fuck. It's cool to know he has a soft side."

Jason nodded and looked away.

"Yeah, he loves his momma. Hey, are you coming to the *Agnostic Front* concert at City Gardens tonight? We could use a ride."

"Aren't the *Circle Jerks* playing too? I'll definitely be there."

"Cool. Do you know if Chris is coming?"

Breezy shrugged her shoulders.

"Who knows?"

"What happened with you two? I thought you were tight."

"We were until he fucked my best friend."

119

"Were you two dating?"

"No. But he knew I liked him. So did Alexis."

"That's fucked up."

Breezy waved it off.

"I don't care. I hope they're happy together."

Jason grinned and nodded.

"I kind of got the impression it was a one night thing. She's not really his type. He likes skinny girls and Alexis is kind of…"

"Fat? Yeah, but she's got big titties and guys like that. That's why Mack was always trying to fuck her."

"Yeah, but Chris wants a girl that looks good on his arm. He likes Asian chicks cause he's all into Japanese Anime."

"Whatever. You want something to eat?"

"I thought you'd never ask."

Breezy turned her back to him and threw some meat on the grille.

"So what are you up to?"

Jason shrugged.

"Just hangin' out. I was gonna go see Padre and get some coffee."

"Tell him I said hi."

She flipped the burger patty a few times, slapped some cheese on it then scooped it up and placed it on a bun. There was still oil and blood dripping from the sizzling meat and Jason preferred his well-done but beggars couldn't be choosers. Who knew when he'd get another meal?

"Thanks, Breezy."

He took a bite of the burger then cocked his head and looked at her.

"What?"

"You know, you look kind of hot with your hair that way."

"Oh, stop."

"No, seriously. You do. You look beautiful."

This time she blushed for real.

"Well thanks, Demon. I always thought you were cute."

Jason winked at her.

"That's cause I am."

He flirted with Breezy while he finished his burger. Every time she smiled at him he felt something flutter in his chest. He'd barely noticed her before but now he couldn't take his eyes off her. Even the freckles on her cheeks, her long pointy nose, and the mole on her neck looked beautiful to him. Her huge blue eyes and pale skin made her look like a porcelain doll.

"How come we never hooked up?" he asked her.

"Because you were too busy hooking up with everyone else. Besides, I thought you and Mack might have been hooking up."

"What? You thought I was gay?"

"No. I knew you liked girls. You and Mack were always bringing girls back to the squat. I just thought maybe you liked boys too. I mean, I thought you liked Mack."

Jason laughed. It sounded fake, even to him.

"You're crazy. I love Mack. He's like my brother. But that doesn't mean I want to fuck him. I mean, I tried that gay shit once, with this guy named Phoenix. I knew I wasn't gay the minute he kissed me. I kissed him. I wasn't into it. So, I walked the fuck away. That was it. That ended any confusion I had about my sexuality. I know who I am now."

Breezy held up her hands.

"I was just telling you what I thought. You asked."

"Yeah, I asked."

Jason took the last bite of his burger then stared at Breezy with a goofy smile on his face.

"What?" Breezy asked.

"We should date."

Breezy smiled and her eyes brightened.

"Are you serious?"

"Yup. I'm serious. We should hook up."

She frowned and crossed her arms over her chest.

"You mean date seriously or just hook up?"

Jason took a silver flask from his jacket pocket. He winked at Breezy, uncapped the flask and took a long swig of vodka to wash the taste of the hamburger from his mouth. He swished it around like mouthwash. He'd stolen both the vodka and the flask itself from his stepfather before he left the house this morning. He reached out and grabbed Breezy by the back of her head, snaring his fingers in her dreadlocks, pulling her closer to him and kissing her. After a moment, she returned the kiss, running her fingers through his freshly washed mane of black hair. When they parted, Jason grinned at her and winked again. This time Breezy returned the smile.

"I mean we should date seriously," Jason said.

Breezy kissed him again.

"Okay."

"Good. It's about time."

Breezy looked down at her feet, once again blushing like a school girl.

"Yeah. It's about time."

"I'll see you tonight?" Jason asked.

"I get off at six."

"I'll be here."

Jason wiped his face with his napkin and took another swig from the flask before tucking it back into his jacket. He waved at Breezy as he stepped outside into the chill morning air. He felt good. Breezy did look good and she had a job and a car. Life was looking better already.

There were a few shoppers on the street, braving the thirteen degree temperature. Jason didn't think it was that cold. It had dropped as low as four degrees earlier this week. In comparison, today felt like a trip to the tropics.

A few high school kids and some kids from the College of Performing Arts wandered the streets dressed all in black, wearing black lipstick and nail polish.

"Fucking art fags," Jason whispered to himself. Then he saw the skinheads.

There were only two of them, one big, one small. The big one had a black eye and a busted lip that somehow made him look even scarier. The little one was thick and muscular with a bulging neck. He was unmarred and looked like one of those wannabe badasses with a Napoleon complex... like Jason. He wore a wool cap over his bald head and a red scarf around his neck. They both wore navy green bomber jackets and black Doc Martins. The guys from *The Unrest* usually wore oxblood combat boots. But Unrest or not, they were looking directly at him and grinning like hyenas closing in on a lion cub. They knew who he was and were looking to score some points by taking him down. Jason reached in his jacket for the bike chain. He pulled it out and began wrapping it around his knuckles as they approached.

The two skinheads walked up to Jason, heedless of the bike chain in his hand. One of them had a small pipe wrapped in duct tape. The other was wearing "sap gloves" with powdered lead or steel shot sewn into the knuckles. Jason knew that one shot with either the gloves or the pipe would have rendered him unconscious and helpless. A few more strikes and he'd be brain damaged or dead. This shit was getting serious.

"Recognize us, you piece of shit?"

They were two of the guys he and Mack had fought the other day. The short muscular kid was the one who got away. The big guy hadn't been as lucky.

"We're looking for Mack."

"Never heard of him."

"Bullshit! You were with him! You're that kid they call Demon aren't you? There's a price on your head. You and that nigger of yours."

For a second, Jason considered lying. The last thing he

wanted was to get into a fight with two armed skinheads by himself. But hearing these racist assholes call Mack a nigger raised his blood pressure to boil. Mack would have never let anyone insult Jason. What kind of friend would he be if he let an insult like that go unpunished?

Fuck it. No guts. No glory.

"Yeah, I'm Demon. Who the fuck are you?"

"I'm Sam and this is Ken. We own South Street," the smaller kid said.

Jason smirked. His legs were shaking but he tried to hide it by smiling even wider. He looked up and down the street, hoping to see someone he knew. Hoping to see Mack running to his rescue. But the streets remained nearly deserted except for the art students and high school kids and none of them looked like they would or could fight.

"*You* own South Street? That's funny. I thought we did."

"Who's *we*?" the larger skinhead, Ken, asked. "You and Mack?"

"Who's *we*? You mean you don't know?" Jason felt the adrenaline spike as his body prepared to act. It felt good. Lately, he'd grown addicted to the sensation.

"Don't fuck with me. Who's *we*? You and who?"

The big guy stepped up and poked Jason in the chest. Jason's smirk widened into a malevolent grin. He bounced from one foot to the next and once again scanned the street. This time he was looking for cops.

"*We* is me and Slash."

"Who's Slash?"

"You've never met Slash? Well, let me introduce you!"

Jason whipped the chain across the larger skinhead's face, ripping a huge gash from the left side of his forehead, across the bridge of his nose, to his right cheek. Blood exploded from the guy's face like he'd been shot.

"ARRRRRGHHHH! FUUUCK! MY EYE!!!"

Again, Jason whipped the chain through the air as the

smaller skinhead charged forward with the pipe. The chain cracked across his knuckles causing Sammy to yell and jump back, cursing and swearing, but he still held the pipe.

"Sonuvabitch! You're dead you filthy piece of shit!"

"You want some more?" Jason stepped forward and whipped the chain through the air again. It whistled past Sammy's face, forcing the skinhead to take a few more steps back to avoid getting his face slashed. The little Nazi still brandished the sawed-off hunk of pipe, ready to use it at the first opportunity. Jason knew he had to hurt the guy in order to get away uninjured himself, but Sammy continued to keep his distance.

Ken, the bigger guy, was still holding his bleeding face with both hands and yelling like someone had raped his mother. He pulled one hand away from his eye, revealing a bleeding hole where his baby blue should have been. Stringy optical nerves dangled down his cheek like long dripping red eyelashes. Jason looked down at his chain and there was a bleeding lump attached to the end of it that he could only assume was part of the guy's missing eye.

"YOU RIPPED OUT MY FUCKING EYE! I'M GONNA FUCKING KILL YOU!!!"

Jason whipped the chain again lashing Ken's neck and raising a livid red welt around the big skinhead's throat. Sammy raised his pipe and charged at him. Jason backed up a few steps, whipping the chain once more

"Leave him the fuck alone!" Breezy yelled from the open take-out window of the burger store. The two skinheads turned and yelled at her.

"I'M GONNA FUCKING KILL HIM! HE PUT OUT MY FUCKING EYE!!!" Ken roared.

"Bitch, stay out of this!" Sammy yelled at her, not taking his eyes off of Jason.

Jason turned and ran. Most of the snow that had been on the ground two days ago had melted away or turned to slush. Still, Jason's combat boots slipped and slid as he tried to flee the two skinheads. He glanced behind him and was pleased to see the two skinheads having just as much trouble staying upright. The big bastard with the missing eye went down hard on the concrete and didn't get up. He sat there in the slush with one hand over the ragged orifice where his eye once was. The other one, Sammy, kept coming and he was getting closer.

There were three choices left. Jason could duck into *Zipperheads*, the punk rock clothing store on the next block, and maybe one of the older punks who worked there would jump in and defend him or he could try to make it to Chris's comic book store four blocks away and hope that the skinhead didn't catch him before he got there or he could try to make it to The Gathering Space which was only two blocks away. He just didn't know if Padre would be much of a deterrent. He'd heard that most skins were religious but who knew how much respect they'd have for a priest who worked out of a storefront, ministering to runaways and drug addicts. Still, it was his best bet. He just hoped that Padre was in.

He kicked it into high gear, sprinting the last block despite the threat of a debilitating fall followed by an even more debilitating beatdown. Jason arrived at The Gathering Space completely exhausted and unable to catch his breath. He would have never made it all the way to the comic store. Too many cigarettes.

He slammed through the metal-framed glass door of The Gathering Space, flinging the door wide so hard it hit the wall with a loud bang and shook like it was about to unhinge. Surprisingly, the glass did not break. There was a meeting of some kind going on. Thirteen or fourteen sad-faced adults of various ages sat in a semi-circle facing Father Antonio. They all jumped to their feet except for one woman who covered her head and drew her knees up to her chest.

"Jason! What are you—"

126

The priest's words were cut short by another loud bang as the door was once again shoved open. This time, with even greater force. The glass shattered but the safety coating held all the broken shards in place so that it looked like an intricate spiderweb.

"You're dead!" the skinhead said, stomping toward Jason with a snarl on his face. His finger jabbed the air like a weapon. In his other hand, he still held the pipe. Jason wielded his chain, ready to swing.

Father Antonio hurried to insert himself between the two teenagers.

"Hold on! What's going on here?"

"This guy and his partner attacked me!" Jason yelled.

"He put my friend's eye out with that chain!"

The skinhead was out of breath as well and yelling only made it worse. He leaned against the wall, struggling to suck air into his overtaxed lungs. Jason stepped forward with the chain but Father Antonio pushed him back.

"No fighting in here or I swear I'll call the cops!"

A couple of the sad sacks of shit who'd been pouring out their souls to the young priest had found their nuts and were now backing him up.

"Yeah, get out of here!"

"I'm not going anywhere! I came to see Padre... I mean, Father Antonio. I always come here. He's the sonuvabitch that don't belong here!"

"Everyone is welcome here. If he wants to stay, he can stay. But no fighting in here and you'll both have to give up your weapons."

The young priest folded his arms then held out his hand for the skinhead's pipe. The skinhead looked at him and snorted then spat on the floor.

"I ain't givin' you shit!" He pointed at Jason. "I'll be waiting for you, outside."

"You'd better see to your friend. He didn't look so good."

The skinhead jabbed his finger at Jason again and raised the pipe.

"Fuck you!"

"Fuck you!"

Jason held up the chain. It was still wet with blood. There was a long stalemate. Finally, the skinhead flipped both middle fingers at Jason then turned and opened the door.

"I'll see you again. Bet on that!" He spit on the floor again before walking out and slamming the door behind him, causing it to crack even more.

"Sorry about that, Padre," Jason said. "I didn't mean for that to happen."

"You want me to call the police? Did he hurt you?"

"No. I'm fine and I'd prefer you didn't call the cops. I've got warrants… uh… some unpaid speeding tickets."

"You don't even own a car."

Jason smirked.

"Let's just call them traffic tickets, okay?"

He walked over to the coffee machine and pulled out a pack of cigarettes, lighting one up while he poured himself a cup. Everyone else walked back to their seats.

"You're welcome to join us if you like."

Jason frowned.

"What is it?"

"Alcoholics Anonymous."

Jason shook his head.

"I'm not an alcoholic."

There were a few chuckles and scoffs. Padre nodded, trying his best to look understanding and suppress the knowing grin spreading across his face.

"Okay, then just listen. Alright?"

Jason looked at the front door. That skinhead might still be out there waiting for him. He walked over and took a seat with the others.

"Fine. I can listen."

TWENTY

Mack's house 1:05 pm

"I know I just postponed my admission until the fall, but I changed my mind. I would really like to come earlier if that's at all possible. I know, but I need to get out of Philly now. No, I'm not in any legal trouble. There's just a lot violence going on in my neighborhood and I'm afraid that if I don't get out now I'll never get out. Yes, ma'am. If you could mail them to me. I'll sign all my financial aid papers as soon as I get them. Yes, the address is the same. Thanks you so much. How soon can I come? Okay, I'll see you then and thanks again."

Mack's mother sat beside him with her hands clasped in prayer. When he hung up the phone, she turned toward him with one eyebrow raised.

"So?"

"They said I can come in two weeks as long as I get all my financial aid papers signed and returned by then."

His mother smiled and stared up at the ceiling, spreading her arms wide like she was hugging the air.

"Oh, thank you, Jesus!" she said, once more clasping her hands in front of her and bowing her head."

"Now, I want you to stay right here, in this house until you leave for college. No more going down to South Street."

"I can't. Not yet anyway. There's people down there that depend on me."

"Those crazy white kids you hang out with? They'll be fine."

Mack shook his head.

"I can't, Mom. I'm sorry. I can't. Just a few more days. I need a few days to wrap some things up."

His mother looked at him again. Tears welled up in her eyes.

"I don't want to lose you. You're my only son and you're about to become the first member of our family to go to college... ever. Do you know how special that is? Your whole world is about to change. Your entire future is ahead of you and it could be something really incredible. You can do incredible things with your life but not if you stay here on these streets. Not if you get arrested and thrown in prison over some dumb shit. Stay here. Don't go down there again. Do it for me. Do it for your old momma."

Mack nodded.

"Just this one last time. I have to go tonight but that's it. I'll stay here 'til I leave for college, okay? But I have to go out tonight. I need to say goodbye to everyone."

Mack picked up his leather coat and sat down on the couch to pull his boots back on.

"Where are you going now?"

"I have to go see Miranda. She's still in the hospital. I need to tell her I'm going."

The stairs squeaked. Mack and his mother both turned to see Jonas coming down the stairs. Jonas was eight years older than Mack's mother and his neatly trimmed beard was almost white. He had crow's feet in the corner of each eye. His pupils were gray like a wolf. He was a large man with a wide chest, broad shoulders, and a huge belly that hung over his belt. He looked like a cross between Paul Bunyon and Santa Claus.

He stepped between Mack and his mother.

"Florence, let me talk to him."

Mack rolled his eyes. He knew the man meant well. Jonas had a good heart. But he hated when Jonas tried to be some kind of male role model or father-figure to Mack. It made him want to knock Jonas' teeth down his throat.

"Christ! When did he get here?"

"He came back this morning, when you were still sleeping."

"Let's talk, Mack, man to man."

Jonas wrapped an arm around Mack's shoulders but Mack shrugged it off.

"Jonas. Don't."

"Mack, I know I'm not your father…"

"Jonas, seriously man, don't."

"Your mom is worried about you and so am I."

Mack cupped his face in his hands, sliding both hands down his cheeks. He looked up at the ceiling and shook his head.

"Jonas, man, this ain't none of your business."

"You're going to get yourself killed out there or wind up in prison. You still carrying that knife?"

"Of course."

"What do you need that for as big as you are?"

"Because some people carry guns and you only got one shot if someone pulls a gun on you."

"Why would you hang out somewhere where someone might pull a gun on you? Come on. You don't need that. You're just going to wind up getting arrested."

"Better tried by twelve than carried by six."

Jonas wrinkled his brow.

"What is that supposed to mean?"

"It means that I'd rather be in jail than dead."

"Why go places where you have to make that choice?"

Mack looked at him like he had lost his mind.

"Where can I go in Philly where I won't have to make that choice? Have you seen this neighborhood? You walk from the front door to the car and back, so you never see what I see. Every time I walk out that door I might have to make that choice. You don't have a clue. I've got to go."

"Mack…"

Jonas reached out for Mack's arm but Mack shrugged him off.

"I said, I'm out of here. I'll be back tomorrow night."

Mack stood up and walked to the front door. He paused and kissed his mother goodbye.

"I love you, Mom. Don't worry about me. I'll be okay."

She held out a scarf and Mack knelt and allowed her to tie it around his neck.

"You should be wearing a hat too. You'll freeze to death out there."

"I'm okay, Mom. Thanks."

She grabbed him and hugged him tight. It felt like more than a goodbye hug. It felt like she was saying goodbye forever. He heard her sob against his chest and something inside him wrenched. He never could stand the thought of hurting her. Even as a young child his mother never had to hit him or yell at him. Just letting him know he'd disappointed her, he'd upset her, had been enough. Things hadn't changed much.

"You come back home, Mack. Do you hear me? No matter what, you come back home."

Mack nodded. He let her go and wiped a tear from her eye with his thumb.

"I will, Mom. I promise. I'll come home. No matter what, I'll be back."

"Mack, wait. I want to give you something."

Jonas reached in his pocket, pulled out his wallet, and fished out two hundred dollar bills and a fifty. He handed them to Mack. Mack looked at the money like it was something that had floated up from a toilet.

"What's this for?"

"For college. You're gonna be on your own for the first time and you'll have expenses. Just take it."

Mack hated when Jonas did shit like this. His generosity

made it hard to hate him.

"Thanks, man. But you really don't have to do this. I'll be alright. I don't leave for two weeks."

"Well, you might need some things before you leave."

Jonas put both hands on Mack's shoulders and pulled him into a hug. Mack rolled his eyes but didn't resist.

Why does he always have to take it too far?

TWENTY-ONE

Bo's apartment, 1:25 pm

Someone was banging on the front door. It sounded like they were using a battering ram. All the hairs on Bo's neck and forearms stood on end.

Fuck. It's the police!

His stomach roiled and his eyes watered as he imagined being handcuffed and dragged off to prison.

"Who the fuck is that?" Gia asked.

Bo crept to the door, trying not to make any sound that might alert whoever was on the other side of the door to his presence. He reached the door and knelt to peer through the peephole. All he could see was a pale, clean-shaven scalp just below the level of the peep hole.

Fuckin' Little Davey.

"What the hell are you doing banging on my door like that, man? I thought you were the police."

Bo unlocked the door and let Little Davey in. He stormed in and began pacing back and forth. He looked like he was about to scream or cry or both.

"Did you hear about what happened to Skinner?"

"Yeah."

"His mom called my house. She said it was our fault!"

Bo shoved his hands in his front pockets and shrugged his shoulders.

"She called my house too. Freaked me out. You think she's right?"

Davey turned toward Bo with homicide twinkling in his eyes like true love.

"It wasn't our fault. It was those fucking jungle-bunnies, those crack-smoking gangbangers!"

Little Davey opened his mouth to speak again then took a quick look down the hall at Bo's open bedroom door.

"Is Gia here?"

"Yeah, she's in bed."

"Hi Davey!"

"Hi Gia!"

Little Davey looked at Bo.

"Let's finish talking outside. Get dressed. I've got something to show you."

Bo hesitated. He looked down the hall at his bedroom, feeling like he should race back into Gia's arms, grow his hair out, and donate his Doc Martins and his bomber jacket to Goodwill. Gia was right. He *was* getting too old for this. He would be twenty soon. He was old enough to vote, old enough to fight for his country, soon he'd be old enough to drink legally. Soon, he'd be old enough to run for public office.

I'd be better off forgetting about fighting niggers in the streets and just become a Republican like every other racist in America, Bo thought. *Not that all Republicans are racists but I've never met a racist that wasn't a Republican. I'd probably do a helluva lot more damage at the ballot box than I've done out here running around with Skinner and Davey.*

Something told him that going outside with Little Davey, hearing whatever he had to tell him, seeing whatever he had to show him, would be the worst mistake of his life. Perhaps it was the fact that Little Davey had done some crazy shit lately, first torching that old black lady and then stabbing that faggot. Perhaps it was because it was open season on skinheads these days. Two skinheads were dead in as many days and the punks in Philly were kicking the shit out of skinheads on site. Or perhaps it was the murderous glee in

Davey's voice when he told him he wanted to show him something outside, that twinkle in his eyes like a kid on Christmas morning. It didn't fit the circumstances. It meant that Little Davey had done something that he was proud of and whatever it was, it had something to do with Skinner. Bo's mind was spinning, trying to figure out what new act of mayhem the little sociopath could possibly have committed. Then his curiosity got the better of him. He grabbed his jacket.

"I'll be back, Gia. I'm just gonna step outside for a minute."

"Wait!"

Gia ran down the hall and into the living room with a tan sheet and a red and white plaid blanket wrapped around her. She looked worried, like she was about to cry.

"Where are you going?"

"I'm just going to step outside for a minute to talk to Little Davey. I'll be right back."

"Why can't you talk here?"

Her eyes were wide and jittery. Her voice cracked on the verge of tears.

What was she so worried about?

But Bo could feel it to. There was something evil in the air, in the air around Little Davey. He still had that insane smile on his face as he watched the exchange between Bo and his girlfriend.

"Because he needs to show me something outside."

"Then I'm coming too."

She dropped the sheets and reached for her coat. She was wearing nothing but a bra and panties.

"Gia. Put some damn clothes on. It's too cold out there."

Little Davey stepped in front of Gia, turning his back on Bo. His eyes were all over her and it was making Bo uncomfortable and beginning to piss him off. He still had that insane smile on his face.

136

"This is personal business, Gia. You can't come with us. He'll be right back. I promise. Don't worry."

Gia looked at Little Davey and Bo could see something in her snap. That crazy look on Davey's face had ratcheted her anxiety up to full panic. Bo knew he needed to step in but a part of him was hoping she would talk Davey out of whatever he was about to get Bo involved in. She pushed past Davey, still in her underwear, and confronted Bo again.

"No! Bo, don't go. Just stay here with me. Don't go with him, Bo. Something's not right and you know it!"

She waved a finger in Bo's face then pointed it directly at Little Davey, emphasizing the mad expression on his face to punctuate her point. Bo gathered her in his arms and kissed her.

"I'll be right back."

He turned and walked out the door with Davey right behind him. He could here Gia weeping as he closed the door. It broke his heart and increased his sense of foreboding. Again, he had the urge to run back inside, back into Gia's arms and forget about Little Davey and the whole skinhead lifestyle and again he fought it.

They walked down the stairs and out to the parking lot. Little Davey's car, his father's car, a big blue and white '59 Ford Fairlane, sat at the far end of the parking lot under a tree by itself. A knot twisted in Bo's gut.

"It's in the car. You're gonna love this!"

Bo stopped walking. He felt like he was about to be sick.

"What's in the car, Davey?"

Little Davey grabbed Bo by his left arm and dragged him forward.

"You'll see. It would ruin the surprise if I told you."

Little Davey fished out the keys as they approached the car. He led Bo around to the trunk. The car shook and Bo's stomach twisted again. He shook his head and backed away.

"Uh uh, Davey. I don't want to see this, man."

137

"See what? You don't even know what I'm about to show you."

But he did know. He knew exactly how Little Davey's mind worked and so did Gia. That's why she'd been so afraid, why she didn't want him to follow Little Davey out to the parking lot.

Little Davey popped open the trunk with a flourish. Just as Bo had suspected, there was a naked black man, gagged and bound with duct tape. His eyes widened and he began thrashing about in the trunk as soon as he saw the two of them staring down at him.

"Shut the fuck up!" Little Davey said then he grabbed the sides of the trunk and lifted himself to kick and stomp the guy a few times until he stopped squirming. Bo looked over his shoulder to make sure no one was watching them. The parking lot was empty. Everyone was either at work or inside their apartments avoiding the cold.

The guy in the trunk had a tapered "block" haircut that leaned to one side like Gumby. It had lines, lightning bolts, and a big money sign cut into it. He wore a gold crucifix in his left ear. Bo was surprised that Little Davey hadn't already ripped the earring out. There were a few cuts and bruises on the guy but nothing like what Bo would have expected Davey to do to him. That only meant one thing, he was saving the worst of it for later. He was saving him for Bo.

"Jesus Christ, man! Who is he?"

"You mean Gumby? He's one of the niggers that killed Skinner. There were three of 'em. The police kept two of 'em and let this one go. They let him go right while I was standing there, trying to get one of the detectives to talk to me. Can you believe that? I followed him from the station and forced him to get in the car."

The guy was kind of big. Bo looked at him and then at Little Davey.

"How'd you get him in the trunk? How'd you get his

138

fucking clothes off?"

"With this!"

Little Davey lifted his jacket to show the Colt revolver in the waistband of his jeans, tucked behind his vintage Nazi SS belt buckle.

"What are you going to do with him?"

Little Davey scowled.

"What the fuck do you think? We're going to torture his ass then burn him up like the old lady in the train station."

The man's eyes flew open and he began to squirm and yell against the duct tape secured around his mouth. His muffled screams and terror-stricken expression sent chills up Bo's spine.

"How do you know he did it? Maybe the cops let him go because he didn't have shit to do with it. How do you know that he was even one of them? Did they say or did you just grab the first black guy that walked out?"

There was brief moment of confusion on Little Davey's face, a moment of doubt then his face filled with rage.

"No, this fucking coon did it, him and those other niggers, and we're going to make him pay. For Skinner. Now get in the car!"

Bo wrinkled his brow and grimaced. He slowly shook his head.

"I'm not getting in that car with you. I've got Gia upstairs waiting for me.

Little Davey put one hand on the gun in his waistband and grabbed Bo's arm with the other. Bo wasn't sure if it was meant to be a threat or if grabbing the pistol was just a reflex.

"Get in the damn car before somebody sees us!"

Little Davey shoved Bo toward the car then jumped behind the wheel and slammed the driver-side door. Bo stood outside the car with his hand on the door handle, trying to decide what to do. He looked up at his apartment window. He thought he could see Gia peering out at him.

"Get in the fucking car!"

Bo took a deep breath then opened the car door and slipped inside. Little Davey gunned the engine, backed out of the parking space, then took off out of the parking lot.

"Where are we going?"

"To the woods. The Unrest is having a meeting in the woods behind the old high school."

"You can't do this at the meeting. Somebody might say something, tell the cops. Just because they're our brothers doesn't mean they can all be trusted with some shit like this. Do you know how many years you'd get for kidnapping?"

"You mean, how many years *we'd* get. And we aren't just kidnapping him. He dies today. But don't worry, the meeting isn't until four o'clock. He'll be dead and buried by then. Nobody will know anything except you and me."

Little Davey looked at Bo for a long moment. His eyes weren't on the road and he didn't say anything. He just stared into Bo's eyes, reading his face, like he was waiting for him to say something, to confess, like he was trying to look into his brain. Bo squirmed uncomfortably but kept his mouth closed. Little Davey slowly turned his eyes back to the road.

I am so fucked, Bo thought. *Why didn't I stay in the apartment with Gia? I knew some shit like this was gonna happen. My life is over.*

They drove toward the high school with Bo shivering in his seat, imagining being gang-raped by big black muscular convicts before finally getting shanked in the shower or being led to the gas chamber. He looked out at the road as it rushed out, wondering how much damage he'd take if he jumped out of the speeding vehicle. He looked at the gun in Little Davey's waistband. Davey's hand was still on the butt. Bo wondered if he could get the gun away from him without being shot.

Then what? Shoot him? Turn him in to the police and save one of the guys that murdered Skinner? The entire

Unrest would be after him if he did something that stupid. Like it or not, he was stuck.

I am so very fucked.

TWENTY-TWO

Einstein Medical Center, 2:15 pm

Mack took the bus to Broad Street and Erie Avenue, to Einstein Medical Center where Miranda was still being treated. It had been days since he'd last seen her. He needed to say goodbye, make sure she was okay, before he left for college and before he went to the concert at City Gardens where he was certain The Unrest would be looking for him and Jason. One way or the other, this might be the last time he saw her.

Mack remembered the money Jonas gave him. He spent two dollars of it to ride the bus. That left two hundred and forty-eight dollars. He still couldn't understand why Jonas gave him the money. *Was he trying to make me feel guilty so I would stay home or is he just trying to impress my mom so she won't throw his ass out again?* Mack wondered. He'd gone through all the money he made during the summer, buying beer for Jason and the rest of his friends. He would have gone to Ohio without a dime in his pocket if Jonas hadn't been so generous. Mack took the money out and counted it before stuffing it back in his pocket. He looked down the block and then across the street at the hospital. He smiled and warmth spread through his cheeks, as an idea took hold of him.

The Einstein Medical Center took up more than a block, stretching from Erie Avenue down to the next block. It was one of the first hospitals in the country to perform heart transplants and boasted some of the best specialists in the country from every discipline. But instead of crossing the street to the hospital, Mack took a left down Broad Street

142

toward the retail shops. He walked another two blocks before he found what he was looking for.

An old jewelry pawn shop called Hechtman's stood between a music shop and a pizza joint. The window looked like a burglar's dream. It was filled with gold necklaces, watches, bracelets, and diamond rings. There were scratches on the glass from where someone had tried to smash through it. The glass must have been thick as hell.

Mack walked in. There was a locked iron security gate beyond the door and Mack had to press a doorbell and wait for the shop owner to look him over before buzzing him in. Mack didn't know what the guy was looking for. He doubted that anyone ever walked up to the gate wearing a ski mask and carrying a shotgun. He wondered who Mr. Hechtman didn't let in if anyone.

Mr. Hechtman was probably in his late sixties. He wore a blue cardigan over a white shirt ala Mr. Rogers and had thick horn-rimmed bifocals and a white mustache that twirled up on the corners. His jewelry store/ pawn shop had been there as long as Mack could remember. He'd come in here with his mom on several occasions and suspected that more than a few of his birthday presents had come from the old store, including the onyx ring he'd received for his eighteenth birthday and the gold necklace his mother had given him for a graduation present.

"How can I help you?"

"I need a ring."

"What kind of ring?"

Mack looked down at one of the display cases at an array of big, gaudy, long out-of-date styles with rubies, opals, sapphires, diamonds or emeralds in them. Most of them looked like something his grandmother would have worn. There was a big display of engagement rings and Mack pointed to one small diamond solitaire with a plain gold band.

143

"How about that one? How much is it?"

"That's a quarter carat, Marquis cut, diamond solitaire with a 24 carat gold band."

"How much?"

"Three hundred dollars."

"I've got two hundred."

Mr. Hechtman, at least that's who Mack assumed he was, looked at Mack then smiled and nodded his head.

"I'll let you have it for two hundred and fifty."

Mack dug in his pocket, pulled out his wallet and removed all the cash he had except for ten dollars to get into the show. He slapped it down on the counter.

`"This is all I've got."

Mr. Hechtman counted the cash. Two hundred and thirty eight dollars. He looked Mack up and down as if appraising his worth. For a moment, Mack was afraid the old guy was going to proposition him for sex or something.

"You love this girl?"

Mack nodded.

"Yes, sir."

The old man raised an eyebrow.

"Is she pregnant?"

"No, sir. She's in the hospital. She's in a coma."

The old man looked down at the ring and nodded again.

"Okay. You've got yourself a deal. But here. You're going to need a really nice case. You want to make a good first impression. What do you think of this one?"

He pulled out a small white satin box trimmed in what looked like gold. He put the ring inside it and handed it to Mack. He scooped the cash off the counter and quickly separated the twenties from the ones and fives, sliding the bills into their slots in the cash register.

"Good luck."

"Thanks, Mister."

Mack left the store. The air felt crisper, colder, refreshing rather than bitter. It smelled fresh despite the glut of cars racing down Broad Street, belching exhaust fumes and the inconsiderate smokers blowing out nicotine clouds as they hurried past. Mack couldn't stop grinning as he walked toward the hospital. There were butterflies in his stomach. He only hoped that Miranda was awake.

Finding his way to the Brain Trauma Unit was more difficult than expected. No one at the hospital seemed to know where it was and he kept getting sent down long hallways that lead to nowhere. After finally making his way to the recovery ward he was told by the nurses that Miranda had been moved to the Moss Rehabilitation Research Institute on Tabor Road. After another bus ride, he finally found her.

Mack stood at the nurse's station with the ring in his pocket, wishing he had brought flowers and feeling foolish for even thinking about it. He was told where to find her by the first nurse he asked, a woman in her thirties with red hair and huge breasts that Mack couldn't stop staring at. He thanked her for the directions but he hesitated. She smiled at him.

"Is there something else?"

Mack finally dropped his eyes from her breasts and stared at the floor. His face twisted and contorted as if he was in pain, which he was. It felt like he'd been gut shot. He had been planning to sit by her bedside and talk to her while she sat in a coma. It would be easier to declare his love to a woman who couldn't talk back, who couldn't reject him. If she was awake, that would change everything.

"Um… uh… is she… is she awake?"

The nurse smiled.

"It's not that simple. She's not completely unconscious but she's not completely conscious either. She comes in and out. Go see her."

Mack didn't move.

"Ma'am? Um… what do you mean she goes in and out?"

145

The nurse smiled sympathetically and put a hand on Mack's shoulder.

"She had a lot of swelling on her brain. That swelling has gone down a lot but she suffered some brain damage as a result. She has opened her eyes and she speaks occasionally but then she lapses back into a comatose state."

Mack looked stricken. Tears welled in his eyes.

"How often is she… conscious? How often does she speak?"

"Every hour or two. Sometimes more often. Sometimes not for an entire day. Go see her. Talk to her. It might help her to hear a friendly voice."

"Are her parents here?"

"They were. I believe they left this morning. They'll probably be back this evening. They've been here every day since the accident. Come with me. I'll show you to her room."

The nurse walked him to where Miranda lay in bed. The bed was adjusted so that she was sitting upright. Her eyes were open but glassy and unfocused. She didn't appear to be conscious at all. Her eyes didn't follow him as he walked toward her. They remained fixed in place. The bruises and cuts on her face had mostly healed and faded to yellowing scars, some of which would probably remain with her for life. She was still remarkably beautiful. It made Mack's heart ache to look at her.

"Miranda?"

"I'll leave you two alone."

The nurse backed slowly out of the room, leaving Mack and Miranda by themselves, surrounded by flower baskets, get-well cards and stuffed toys. Mack leaned in and kissed Miranda on the cheek.

"I love you, Miranda," he said without hesitation. "I've loved you for as long as I've known you. Please come back."

Miranda continued staring straight ahead, eyes fixed in

place. Mack fished in his pocket for the ring. He held the little satin-covered box in his hands, staring down at it while he spoke.

"There's going to be a big brawl tonight. Me and Jason have been kicking the shit out of The Unrest since you've been in the hospital. They're all gunning for us now. They're probably going to be at the concert tonight at City Gardens. If they're there, it's going to get pretty bloody. I might wind up in here right next to you. Either that or in the morgue."

He looked up at her and was startled to see that she was looking at him.

"Miranda? Can you hear me?"

She didn't reply or give any indication that she'd heard him, no indication that she was aware of him at all except that her head was now turned toward him. Her eyes remained fixed but they were now fixed on him. It was a good sign though it was more than a little disturbing. Mack reached out and stroked her cheek with the back of his hand. Her eyes never wavered. He brushed her other cheek then leaned in and kissed her forehead. A tear left his eye and trickled down his cheek. He quickly wiped it away. When he spoke, his voice wavered.

"I- I'm going to be leaving for college in two weeks. I've got to get out of Philly... for a few reasons. But I just couldn't leave without saying goodbye and telling you how I felt."

"Mack?"

She was awake. Her eyes were now fully focused. She blinked several times then smiled.

"Mack, you came."

It was one of those moments of consciousness the nurse told him about and it couldn't have come at a more awkward time.

"Miranda, I..." he swallowed hard. "I love you and..." he opened the little box and took out the ring. He took her

147

hand and slid the ring on her finger. "I want you to marry me."

"I love you too, Mack."

That was all she said. She slipped out of consciousness again. But this time, there was a smile on her face.

"I'll be back, Miranda. I'm going to marry you."

He kissed her again before he left. This time, he kissed her on the lips.

"I'll be back."

TWENTY-THREE

The woods, 3:00 pm

The black guy with the block "Gumby" haircut lay in ruins. Little Davey had scalped the guy. He'd taken his bowie knife, grabbed the man by his hair, then cut into his forehead and scraped the blade along Gumby's skull, removing his skin along with his ridiculous hair. His scalp was now flipped back, hanging off the base of his skull like a hood, revealing the gleaming white bone of his bleeding cranium.

Bo had always known that Davey was crazy. But this went far beyond the normal teenaged insanity. This was the type of crazy that led to dead hookers buried in the basement. Little Davey began cutting off Gumby's fingers next, pausing occasionally to punch or stomp the man as he hacked and sawed through each of his digits while Bo held the guy down. Bo kept looking around to make sure no one was coming, almost hoping that someone would stop them.

The man regained consciousness while Little Davey was still sawing through his thumb with the big bowie knife. He began screaming and thrashing so hard Bo was having a hard time holding him. Davey started punching him again, trying to silence him. Blood was flying everywhere as the blows sent the man's scalp flopping back and forth. Gumby's scalp slapped Bo in the face with a wet "Thwap!" as he tried to hold him down. It was too much.

"Stop it, Davey! That's it! That's enough, man! Let's just kill him and bury his body. I can't stand this no more. I'm gonna be sick."

Bo felt the bile rise, burning in his throat, and had to

swallow hard to keep it from coming up. His skin looked even paler than normal.

"Come on, man. Don't be such a pussy! We've got to cut his fingers off anyway so they can't fingerprint him and identify the body. I'm almost done. You need to remember what this bastard did to Skinner. We've got to make him pay!"

"Look at him, Davey! He's paid enough. Let's put him out of his misery."

"Uh uh. No way. This piece of shit has got a lot more suffering to do. He killed one of ours! He murdered Skinner, dude!"

Little Davey jabbed the Bowie knife into the man's face and began sawing off his nose as he spoke to Bo which brought a volley of bloodcurdling screams from their captive, audible even through the duct tape around his mouth. Inky blackish red blood and fluid rained down the man's face. Bo turned his head to keep from throwing up, but began to retch as the grating sound of the knife sawing through cartilage surrounded him. Spots danced in front of his eyes.

"Give me the gun."

"What?"

"Give me the fucking gun!"

Little Davey handed Bo the gun. Bo placed the gun to the black guy's temple.

"Not yet, dude. Not next to my fucking car!!!"

Bo pulled the trigger but nothing happened.

"Dude, the gun is empty. I've only got like twelve bullets and I'm saving those for tonight. I ain't wasting no bullets on this piece of shit."

Little Davey began sawing off one of the guy's biceps. He slid the knife down the man's humerus, slicing the muscle free from the bone while the man thrashed and bucked and screamed for his fleeting life. Bo turned away.

"I can't believe you're this fucking squeamish, Bo. Did

you know that they used to skin niggers alive and set them on fire at fucking picnics? They would tie them to a tree and cut on them then they'd douse them in gasoline and light 'em up. Women would come out to watch it with their kids. They used to do it to runaway slaves and then later the Klan did it to niggers who raped white women. Families would sit out on the grass eating and drinking and watching niggers burn. The kids would even take trophies. That's where they got the name "picnic" from. They used to call it "pick-a-nigger" because the kids would run up and snag an ear or a toe or a finger or something as a souvenir. It's true. I read it in a book. And here you are, a grown man, and you can't even watch the guy who murdered one of your best friends get what he deserves? That's fucking pathetic, dude. Doesn't that bother you? Don't you think there's something wrong about that?"

But Bo was in no condition to answer. He was on his knees, vomiting his last meal onto the forest floor.

Davey stopped sawing on the man's arm and grabbed Gumby's bicep with both hands. He put his foot on the guy's forearm for leverage then yanked the muscle free with a wet sticky "Riiiiiip!" that sent Bo into a fresh volley of projectile vomiting.

"Bo, dude, will you stop being such a pussy! It ain't that bad. The guy passed out. He didn't even feel it. It's pretty funny actually."

But Bo couldn't think of anything remotely funny about it and it worried him that Little Davey could find any humor in this at all. Bo looked into the black guy's dying eyes and for the first time since the ninth grade, he didn't see a nigger, didn't see an enemy. All he saw in those eyes was another human being… suffering. And Little Davey wasn't finished with him yet.

TWENTY-FOUR

South Street, 4:16pm

Jason left The Gathering Space shaken. He shook hands with Padre and the other "Twelve-Step" members and wandered off down the street. He'd sat through two AA meetings in a row. He felt drained but more than that, he felt reborn. Padre was right. He was an alcoholic. He'd started drinking at fourteen and hadn't spent a single evening sober since. But he now knew that there were people to help him. There was hope.

"Thanks for everything, Padre. You don't know how much I appreciate it. I guess I've got some work to do."

Father Antonio smiled.

"One day at a time, Jason. You'll get there. One day at a time."

Jason winced. He still hated those fucking slogans. It made them all sound brainwashed but perhaps that's what it took. He just didn't know if he can get behind the idea of giving his life over to a higher power the way Padre recommended. He didn't believe in a god of any kind. He was pretty sure that there was no intelligent creator and if there was one, he was certain that god didn't care two shits for him or anyone else on earth. So who was there for him to pray for? That was going to be a pretty hard obstacle for him to overcome. If the creator wasn't his higher power than what was?

Love? Pussy? Mack?

"Mack?"

Mack was walking up South Street looking sad. It was

152

rare to see Mack without a smile on his face so his expression immediately worried Jason. Something must be really wrong.

"Hey, Demon."

"What's up, Mack? You okay, dude? Is it Miranda? Did something happen?"

Bo nodded slowly, still looking down at the pavement. Jason tried to make eye contact without success.

"I proposed to her."

"You fucking did what?"

Mack looked up and met Jason's concerned gaze.

"I asked Miranda to marry me."

Jason smiled and slapped Mack on the arm.

"Dude, you're fucking crazy! What did she say?"

Mack shrugged.

"Nothing. She slipped back into a coma, but she did say she loved me too."

Jason wanted to tell Mack that he was out of his fucking mind, that he was too young and there was too much great pussy out there to be had to get tied down so soon, but he could see that Mack was troubled so he held his opinions.

"She'll be fine, man. You'll see. It's a good sign that she was awake at all."

Mack nodded but he looked anything but convinced.

"They said the swelling had gone down. They're giving her some kind of hypothermia treatment. Using cold baths to wake her up. It looked like it was working… kind of."

Jason turned the collar of his leather jacket up against the cold, shoved his hands in his pocket, and stomped in place, trying to warm himself.

"She'll come around. Einstein is one of the best hospitals in the country."

Mack nodded again and that's when Jason noticed the swelling around his eyes and his split lip.

"What the fuck happened to your face?"

"I got jumped by a bunch of skinheads on the train

yesterday. They almost killed me. I stabbed one of 'em. This shit is getting pretty serious."

"I got attacked too. They said The Unrest put a bounty on our heads."

"Who said that?"

"These two skinheads. I put out one of their eyes with my chain."

Jason held up the chain so Mack could see it. There were still flecks of dried blood on it. Mack's face grew more solemn.

"We need to talk, man."

Mack led Jason back into The Gathering Space and the two of them took a seat on one of the couches. Father Antonio waved and Mack waved back but didn't speak, turning his back on the priest and focusing his attention on Jason. Jason felt immediately uncomfortable. There was a stiffness to Mack's posture and a seriousness in his expression that looked out of place. It frightened Jason more than a little.

"What's up, dude?"

"Demon, I've got to get out of Philly... I'm leaving for college in two weeks. This is probably going to be the last time you see me down here for a while."

Jason felt his stomach twist. His vision narrowed until all he could see was Mack's face as if he was staring at it from the end of a long tunnel.

"What? Why?"

Mack drew in a deep breath.

"Because if I stay here much longer I'm gonna wind up either dead or in prison. Both of us will."

Jason couldn't breathe.

"What about Miranda?"

Mack shrugged.

"I know. That's the hard part. You and her and my mom are the only people in this shit-hole I'm really going to miss. If she wakes up and she wants to marry me then I'll send for her. They have dorms on campus for married couples."

"You're serious about this."

"Yeah. I already promised my mom that I was going."

Jason knew what that meant.

"Then I guess it's done. I know you ain't gonna go back on a promise to you mom and I ain't gonna ask you to. You know The Unrest is gonna kill me once you're gone though, right? I'm a dead man as soon as they find out you're not around."

A look passed Mack's face that Jason had seen many times in the past. His features hardened, becoming more stern, more determined. It was his battle face.

"They won't get you. Nobody's gonna kill you. Not if we get to them first. That's going to be my parting gift to you before I leave. We're going to war with the entire fucking Unrest. We're gonna end this shit. Tonight! Call every punk you know from the scene and tell them to meet us at City Gardens tonight."

"You gonna kill them all? Is that your plan? That's fucking crazy and fucking impossible."

Mack nodded and smiled.

"I don't have to kill them all. You know how you kill a snake? You cut its head off. That's what I'm gonna do. I'm gonna cut the head off the fucking snake."

TWENTY-FIVE

The woods, 5:49 pm

"White Power! White Power! White Power!"

John Jones had just finished speaking. He'd managed to whip the crowd of nearly a hundred into a murderous frenzy. They were ready for war.

An army of clean-shaven men, boys, and even young women, from fourteen to their mid-twenties, filled the woods behind the high school mere yards from where Bo and Little Davey had just buried the mutilated remains of a guy they believed to be responsible for their friend's death. In a final act of cruelty, Little Davey had castrated the man while the murdering fuck screamed himself hoarse. The man barely had any energy left but he'd come alive when Little Davey began sawing through his dick. He thrashed and screamed like a wet cat on an electric fence. Then Davey cut the man's throat from one side of his jaw to the other, jugular to carotid, nearly decapitating him. He looked like a gore-soaked PEZ dispenser. Little Davey then shoved the man's cock through the gash in his trachea. They dumped him into the pit they'd dug and set him on fire before burying his body. He'd still been alive, drowning in his own blood and choking on his own cock when his skin had begun to blacken and char then to run like taffy as the flames consumed him and his own body fat added grease to the flame. Minutes after they'd finished burying the body, the first of their Unrest brothers had shown up. Soon, the woods were full of them and then John Jones arrived and began to tell them about the coming race war and how they all needed to do their part and that they shouldn't be shy about shedding blood to preserve the race. He had no idea the war had already begun and first blood had already been shed.

"I've got to make a stop before we leave." Little Davey said.

"What? Where are you going?"

"I need to see Cindy."

Bo didn't like that. He didn't trust it. Not one bit.

"Why do you need to see her for?"

"Just to say goodbye. You know, in case something happens tonight."

"Come on, Davey. Just let that shit go. It's over between you two. She doesn't want to see you and in the mood you're in you might do something crazy."

"Something Crazy" was exactly what Little Davey had in mind, but he couldn't tell Bo that. Bo didn't have the stomach for this. He'd shown his yellow streak when they were torturing the spook who killed Skinner. Bo hadn't done shit but help him bury the body. He didn't have the balls for wet work… but Little Davey did. He had big iron King Kong balls and he was going to show Cindy just how much they'd grown.

"You don't have to come if you don't want to. I'll just meet you at City Gardens. I should probably do this myself anyway. I'll see you at the concert."

Bo watched Little Davey walk off toward his car, feeling like he should have said something to stop him, but once again he did nothing. He wasn't sure there was anything he could do except call the police and there was no way he was going to do that. Not after burning that black guy alive. There was too much on his conscience and he doubted he'd stand up well to an interrogation. Instead, he decided to try to call Cindy and warn her. He jogged off in search of a pay phone.

TWENTY-SIX

Breezy's car, Ben Franklin Bridge, 6:30 pm

When it was first built, the Benjamin Franklin Bridge was the largest suspension bridge in the world. A computer-driven lighting system added in the mid-seventies illuminated each cable in succession in a cascading crescendo that made the bridge shimmer like a waterfall. As Bo, Breezy, and Demon traveled across it, a hundred and thirty-five feet above the Delaware River, they were completely oblivious to its wonder and beauty. Their minds were focused on their own individual fears and desires.

The three of them were huddled together on the long bench seat of Breezy's candy apple red, Chevy Nova. They hadn't spoken a word to one another since they left South Street.

Mack finally broke the silence. He plastered a fake smile on his face in a lukewarm effort to lighten the mood.

"So, you two are a couple now? That's really cool."

Breezy turned with a bright and genuine smile lighting up her face. She'd obviously been dying to talk about her new boyfriend.

"Thanks, Mack! Isn't it great? And don't worry about your little Demon. I'll take care of him. I think it's so cool that you're going to college. When are you leaving?"

"The week after next."

Jason snorted but kept his eyes down, averted from Mack.

"Come on, Demon. You know I don't want to leave you guys, but I have to get out of here. Shit has just gotten too

158

hot down here. And we can't live like this forever. You think we're going to be crashing at a squat, picking up teenaged yuppie chicks, going to hardcore shows and fighting skins for the rest of our lives? We've got to grow up sometime and this is my time."

Jason nodded. Mack could see his jaw muscles clenching and unclenching as if he was chewing on something unusually tough.

"I love you, Mack. Just remember that. No matter what happens. You're my boy. You're my family and I'm going to miss you."

"I love you too, Demon. You should get out of here too. There's nothing here in Philly for you either. You should try to get into the same college as me."

"I dropped out of high school, Mack. I never graduated. I dropped out with three months left to go. You think they're going to let me into college now?

He never looked up. There was a hitch in his voice. Breezy placed a hand on his back in concern.

"Why'd you drop out?"

Jason shrugged and exhaled loudly.

"Padre thinks I'm an alcoholic. I went to a couple of meetings today. I don't know. He might be right. I think I'm gonna keep going."

Mack ran a hand over Jason's long mane. Jason turned to look at him. There were tears in his eyes. Mack leaned over and hugged him.

"That's good, man. I think that's real good."

Breezy rubbed the back of Jason's head, looking over his shoulder at Mack. There was an expression of concern on her face.

"So, what happens when we get to City Gardens? You guys aren't just going to watch the concert are you?"

Mack felt Breezy's eyes on him. He released Jason from his embrace, feeling like Breezy was getting jealous or something. He looked down at Jason who was staring at his lap again. He had the bike chain wrapped around his knuckles.

"Lots of pain. That's what happens. Lot of pain." Jason said.

TWENTY-SEVEN

Cindy's house, 6:35 pm

There were two cars in the driveway. Cindy's silver Volkswagen Scirocco and a black Chevy truck Little Davey'd never seen before. Both Cindy's parents were dead and, as far as Little Davey knew, Cindy hadn't taken on any roommates. That meant her boyfriend was in there with her … and his son.

Little Davey pulled his father's revolver out of the glove compartment and began loading it. He was so angry his hands shook. He spilled several bullets onto the floor.

"Fuck!"

He punched the dashboard.

"I'm going to kill this bitch!"

He bent over and searched the floor for the missing bullets, trying desperately to calm himself down enough to load the gun. He found all but one shell, loaded the gun, and stepped out of the truck, onto the sidewalk. He stuck the gun in the small of his back and pulled his jacket down over it. The sun was already setting and there were dark clouds moving in across the sky. A chill wet wind blew through the street and pushed Little Davey back two steps. It felt like it was about to rain or snow. Either way, the freeway would be a mess. He needed to get Mickey and get on the road if he was ever going to make it to the concert.

Little Davey walked up the driveway, paused in front of the black truck, then pulled out his bowie knife. He let out an anguished cry, raised the knife and brought it down hard, puncturing the tire. The tire hissed loudly as it deflated.

Davey wrenched the knife free and moved onto the next tire and the next. He was preparing to stab the last tire when the door opened and a tall Puerto Rican man, wearing baggy, black "Z Cavarricci" pants and a black muscle shirt, came running out of the house. He had thick black hair that flowed in curly locks down to his shoulders like one of those heavy metal dudes, dark tan skin and hazel eyes. He looked like a matinee idol, like Lawrence Olivier. He was fucking beautiful, fucking Puerto Rican, and he was fucking the mother of Little Davey's child.

Davey shook his head and snorted.

"A fucking spic. She left me for a fucking spic," Davey whispered.

"Hey! What the fuck are you doing to my car?"

Little Davey stuck his hand behind his back and grabbed the butt of the pistol. He smiled as he watched the Puerto Rican walk toward him, pointing and yelling. He imagined how satisfying it would feel to put a bullet in the spic's beautiful face and his smile widened.

"Is this your truck?"

"Yeah, it's my fucking truck, you fucking lunatic!"

The Puerto Rican guy came closer, waving his arms in a threatening manner, shouting and yelling. Neighbors were starting to peek out of their windows. Davey wondered if he could shoot the guy and get away with it. If he waited for the guy to swing, he might even be able to claim self-defense.

"I just can't believe this. You? A fucking spic? You're fucking Cindy? You're her new boyfriend?"

Cindy was standing in the doorway now. Just standing there. Not saying anything, not rushing to put herself in between the two men and prevent a physical altercation. She was just watching and waiting as if she wanted them to fight, as if she couldn't wait to see her new boyfriend mop the floor with her crazy ex.

"You? Yeah... you're that fucking skinhead she used

to date. Is that what the fuck this is about? That's why you slashed my fucking tires, maricon?"

"Yup," Davey answered, smiling.

The Puerto Rican guy raised his fist and Davey raised the pistol.

"Hold up, man! Hold up! Wait!"

The Puerto Rican man with the lean muscular build and the light-colored eyes, bow-shaped lips, strong, angular jaw, high cheekbones, perfect white teeth and curly black hair, held up his hands in surrender.

"It's cool, bro. It's cool." The guy said in a calm voice as he tried to back away with his hands raised. Now that Davey was looking at him, the dude looked just like Slash from *Guns n' Roses.* The bastard was beautiful. But he was still a dead man.

"Do I look like your fucking brother?"

"Davey! No!"

Davey shot him once in the abdomen.

"Owww! Fuck! You shot me! Goddamn motherfucker! Help! Somebody help me! I'm shot!"

The man dropped to his knees, holding his bleeding guts. Davey stepped forward and stared into the man's beautiful eyes. He could see what Cindy saw in him. Even with his face contorted in agony, even on his knees, pleading for his life, even with his life fluid bleeding out onto the driveway, he was handsome as fuck. Davey shot him in the face. He didn't look quite as handsome with a third nostril and most of the back of his head missing.

Cindy's screams broke through the haze of rage and madness clouding Davey's thoughts.

"Alvarooooo! Oh, my god! Alvaro! Alvaro!"

She ran down the front steps and onto the driveway where Alvaro lay bleeding from the face and stomach. His skull looked like a shattered eggshell. What looked like a glob of strawberry jam and spaghetti was sprayed across the concrete. Cindy knelt beside it, reaching out for her dead lover. Davey put the gun in her face.

"Don't fucking touch that filthy spic. Get your ass in the house!"

Cindy stared at the barrel of the revolver. Her mouth creaked open and hung there, lips wide, for several seconds before words came out.

"Wh-why are you doing this? Are you going to kill me now? Mickey is in there. Do you want him to see this? He's your son, Davey!"

Little Davey leaned down until his face was inches from hers.

"If you want to die out here next to your wetback boyfriend then keep talking. Get your whoring ass in the house! NOW!"

Cindy rose on legs that shook. When she tried to walk, her legs wobbled like a newborn calf. Little Davey prodded her with the gun. Neighbors had begun coming out of their houses to see what was going on, apparently assuming that he'd shot a mugger or a burglar until they saw him point the gun at Cindy. Davey watched them freeze in their tracks and some of them retreated back into their houses, presumably to call the police.

"Hurry up. Go get my son."

"Don't take him, Davey. Don't take my baby!"

Little Davey grabbed her by the back of the neck, squeezing hard as he pushed her forward and up the stairs into the house.

"Do what the fuck I say and maybe you'll see him again. But if you don't, I promise you, you will die here tonight."

Cindy began sobbing uncontrollably.

"Don't do this. Please, don't do this! Davey, please! Please Davey, don't do this!"

"You should have thought about this before you started fucking that spic in front of my son!"

The coffee table held the remains of a Chinese takeout dinner and several empty bottles of Heineken. It was the only beer Cindy liked and Davey hated the shit. The VCR was on and "Back To The Future" was paused at the scene where Marty was playing guitar at his parents' senior prom. A pink blanket was draped over the couch. At least she hadn't been fucking him in her bed, the one they used to share, the one they had conceived Mickey in. Davey pushed her down on the couch.

"Stay right the fuck there!"

He ran upstairs, taking the steps two at a time despite his small legs. Mickey was sitting up in his crib with his eyes wide. He smiled when Davey walked in. Davey smiled back.

"Hey, sport. You ready to go for a ride with Daddy?"

He scooped him up and snatched some clothes out of a drawer along with some diapers and shoved them all into his diaper bag. He grabbed his son's snowsuit out of the closet. When he turned, Cindy was right behind him, coming at him with a knife. He swung the butt of the gun at her temple. He could feel the impact of the blow all the way up his arm. He'd struck her harder than he'd intended. She fell backwards. Her head struck the scuffed and splintered hardwood floor and bounced. Her eyes rolled up in her head and blood leaked from her nose. The knife skidded across the room and under Mickey's crib. Davey turned back to Mickey who had now begun to cry.

"It's okay, sport. Everything's okay. Mommy's fine. She's just taking a nap. We've got to go now, okay? Let's get dressed."

He left Mickey's pajama's on as he shoved his arms and legs into the snowsuit and hunted through the drawers for socks and gloves. He found them along with a hat and was looking for his son's shoes when Cindy sat up like fucking Michael Meyers in Halloween. He aimed the gun at her and backed up, holding Mickey's hand. Cindy wiped the blood from her nose and stared at it, then she laughed.

"Your dad made you this way. You don't even know if it was really a black guy that your mom ran away with. That could have just been a story your dad told you to justify his racism and make sure you turned out the same damn way. He probably just chased her away with his drinking and his violence, the same way you chased me away."

"You don't know what the fuck you're talking about." Davey said, chuckling. His smile quivered and his gaze roamed the floor, avoiding hers.

"Don't I? You don't sound so sure. And those kids that beat you up in high school. Do you really think it would have been any different if you went to an all-white school? They beat you up because you were different and you were smaller than they were and because kids are fucking cruel. When I was in elementary school I got teased because I was too skinny. Another girl in my class got teased because she was too fat. Kids will attack anyone who's different. It's not a black thing. It's a kid thing. What do you think black kids go through in all white schools? Should they all start shaving their heads and attacking every white guy they see?

"You knew who I was when you met me. Did you think you could change me?"

Cindy nodded.

"That's exactly what I thought. That's what all women think. But I was wrong." Cindy shook her head and chuckled again. "Your dad fucked you up bad. There's no fixing what's wrong with you. And now you've killed someone. You're going to jail for life, Davey. Don't you know that? You killed someone, Davey. You killed my fucking boyfriend!"

Davey cocked the hammer back on the revolver.

"I've killed a lot of people."

Cindy's face looked shocked before he pulled the trigger, then it just looked empty. She was gone, bleeding out on the hardwood floor from the hole in her forehead. The smell of blood and sulfur assaulted his nostrils. Gun smoke seared his eyes. That was the only explanation he could think of for the tears.

Mickey's eyes widened and his body stiffened. He sat there, stiff as a board for a long moment before letting out a loud wailing cry. It sounded like he was in mortal agony.

"Let's go, sport."

Davey raced down the stairs, carrying Mickey and the diaper bag and nearly dropping both of them. He managed to make it to his car and was two blocks away before he heard the first sirens. Several police vehicles raced past him with lights and sirens blaring. Davey let out a long sigh then reached across to rustle his son's hair, laughing while he adjusted the rearview mirror and watched the flashing red and blue lights recede into the distance.

"Those fucking niggers are right. Nine-one-one is a joke."

TWENTY-EIGHT

Trenton, New Jersey, City Gardens night club, 7:45 pm

The off-white, graffiti-covered, single story warehouse sat across the parking lot surrounded by a couple hundred rioting punk rockers and skinheads. A flurry of snowflakes speckled the air with dots of white even as the combatants spattered the concrete with splashes of red. There were no police anywhere, which was unusual for a City Gardens concert. It was as if the Trenton PD were purposely avoiding the place. In the hardcore scene, fights didn't always end when the cops showed up. Often, that's when they got started.

"What's going on?" Breezy shouted as she piloted the Chevy Nova through the parking lot and the crowd of thrashing bodies.

"Park the car! Wait for me!" Mack was already leaping out of the car before it had even come to a complete halt. Jason jumped out behind him. The war had begun without them.

"Where are you going?"

"To cut the head off the fucking snake!" Mack responded.

"What the hell does that mean?"

"It's fucking war, that's what it is!" Jason answered. He swung the bike chain, whipping and slashing his way through the crowd as he followed Mack into the fray.

There were bodies lying in pools of blood, heads split open, noses broken, the distinct impression of the sole of a Doc Marten combat boot imprinted on their faces, moaning, contorting in agony, or completely unconscious. He saw Cat and Simon slashing a couple of skinhead chicks with box cutters. A guy punched Cat high on the head. She staggered, then slashed the guy's forearm and bicep with the box cutter, trying to get to his face.

Mack swung at anything with a bald head. The sound of his knuckles striking flesh could be clearly distinguished even among the other sounds of violence. Twice, Mack was dropped to his knees by punches he didn't see, but he immediately scrambled back to his feet and knocked the shit out of any skinhead within reach. He was knocked onto his back when he tripped over a fallen punk while taking a punch. Chris, from the comic shop helped him to his feet.

"You okay, Bro?"

"I'm fine."

"I've got your back."

Mack nodded.

"Yeah, okay."

Mack was bleeding and swollen within minutes of leaving the Nova. His face was a mask of blood and fury. There were cuts above and beneath both eyes, his knuckles were bleeding and throbbed in pain, so swollen that he could barely make a fist. His jaw hurt, his nose was bleeding and his lip had split wide open but he was still furiously battling, cutting a swath through the crowd, making his way toward John Jones, the head of the most notorious skinhead group in New Jersey, *The Unrest.*

John Jones was just shy of six-feet, built like Arnold Swarzenegger, and covered in tattoos. He looked like the stereotypical image of a serious badass. It was more than an affectation. John Jones was a fucking monster. But Mack was certain that he could take him. He had to take him. It was the only way that his friends would ever be safe from *The Unrest.*

Mack was within twenty feet of John Jones when a big skinhead with a large red beard stepped in front of him and swung a clumsy punch that just missed Mack's jaw. Mack ducked low and slammed his fist into the guy's solar plexus. The blow doubled red-beard over. He backed up, holding his rib cage as Mack moved in to finish him off. Mack kicked at the Nazi's head like he was punting a football. His big, steel-toed motorcycle boot connected with the skinhead's jaw and sent a spray of blood and teeth across the asphalt. Red-beard collapsed, landing face-first onto the hard blacktop. The impact jarred him awake and red-beard staggered back to his feet... and charged.

A punch thudded against Mack's chest, another one caught him high on the cheek and another one popped him in the left eye. The guy was still slow but he had surprised Mack by recovering so quickly. He almost knocked Mack down but Mack drove a knee into red-beard's gut and doubled him over again. This time, Mack threw a quick left hook-right hook- uppercut combination that wilted the big skinhead. When he hit the ground this time, he didn't move. Mack was so enraged that he began kicking the guy as he lay semi-conscious. He stomped down on the skinhead's face again and again until it split and swelled, turning blue and purple and gushing blood from his lacerated mouth, cheeks, forehead, and pulverized nose. He booted him in the side of his head until red-beard's entire skull seemed to swell like one large hematoma, until it looked the way Miranda's looked the day she was beaten by *The Unrest* at *Club Pizzazz*, the day they took her away from him.

"Mack!"

Mack heard Jason's voice and turned just as the gun went off. He felt something punch him in the gut. The second bullet shattered his forearm and Mack cried out in pain. It was the worst pain he'd ever felt. The next struck him in the chest, just below his collarbone. A short, angry little skinhead was pointing a big revolver at him and firing. Jason was charging up behind the skinhead, swinging the bike chain, intent on saving Mack's life. The little skinhead turned seconds before

Jason reached him.

"Demon! Noooo!"

Mack crossed the distance between him and the short skinhead as quickly as he could, but he wasn't quick enough. The pain in his stomach, chest, and forearm slowed him down. The little Nazi fuck got off two shots before Mack tackled him. He saw Jason fall, saw the blood spurt from his chest and head and that mischievous gleam, that devilish spark, wink out in his friend's eye moments before Mack lost consciousness as well.

TWENTY-NINE

Aftermath
Einstein Medical Center, 8:15 am

The sound of his mother weeping woke Mack. The first thing he was aware of, besides the fact that he was in the hospital, was the pain in his arm. He still couldn't feel the chest wound or the wound in his belly, but his arm hurt like hell. It was in a cast and elevated above his chest on some sort of little pulley. No sooner had he awakened in agony then a nurse arrived with a needle full of Demerol. Moments later, the pain in his arm was just a dull memory.

He looked over at his mother. She sat by his bed, weeping. She looked like she had lost weight. Her hair was not done and she wore no makeup, which was almost unheard of for her in public. Jonas was there as well, wearing a stern look of disapproval and disappointment. If his mother wasn't there, Mack would have told him to go fuck himself.

"I'm okay, mom. Don't cry." His voice was hoarse and his lips felt chapped, like he hadn't spoken in days. The nurse, a Korean woman in her thirties, handed him a glass of water and held his head up for him so he could drink. Mack was surprised by how weak he felt. If she hadn't held his head, he wasn't certain he'd have been able to lift it on his own.

His mother scooted closer to him and placed a hand on his chest, over the bandage where he'd been shot. He lifted his arm to stroke her face but it was handcuffed to the bedrail.

"What the hell?"

"Some cops came in and arrested you last night. They

172

say you killed two people the night you got shot."

Mack was puzzled.

Two people?

He remembered stomping that skinhead with the big red beard. He supposed that he may have killed him accidentally. And he remembered tackling the guy who shot him and Jason. But he couldn't have killed that guy. He passed out right after he tackled that little Nazi fuck.

"What two people?"

"After you got shot, you stabbed a guy who is supposed to be the leader of some skinhead group you were fighting with."

"John Jones? I stabbed John Jones? How the hell is that even possible? I was unconscious! I passed out after I got shot."

His mother slowly shook her head.

"The witnesses said that you got shot and then your friend Jason got shot and then you tackled the gunman and knocked the gun out of his hand. He took off running and disappeared into the crowd, then you pulled out a knife and ran across the parking lot and stabbed that John Jones guy about fourteen times. You were sitting on top of his body with the knife still in your hand when the cops came. They almost shot you until they realized that you were unconscious."

Mack's eyes were wide and his mouth hung open. He couldn't believe it.

"I stabbed him fourteen times? That can't be."

He had wanted to kill that bastard so bad and he'd apparently succeeded but he felt none of the satisfaction he should have felt because he couldn't remember any of it.

"You must have been in shock."

"How could I have killed someone and not remember it? So, are they charging me with murder?"

"We're waiting to find out. Right now, they are just holding you as a suspect."

Mack tried to force himself to recall the stabbing. He remembered seeing the big bull of a man covered in white supremacist tattoos and trying to fight his way toward him. He remembered being kicked and punched and nearly knocked unconscious several times as he made his way through the crowd. A six-foot-six black man in a parking lot full of racist skinheads must have been like a beacon. He'd knock down one of the Nazi bastards and another one would leap up to fill his fallen comrades place. They were like cockroaches, but he'd been determined. Every time he was knocked down, he'd gotten up and kept fighting, kept struggling to get to the racist, white supremacist piece of shit that started *The Unrest* and end him.

Killing John Jones was his only reason for going to the concert, but he'd hoped to do it discreetly, in the midst of the riot, disguised by the pandemonium and bloodshed. Apparently, he'd gone buck wild after the shooting and stabbed the man in full view of everyone, in front of more than a hundred witnesses. Instead of stealthily sliding the knife up between the skinhead's ribcage and disappearing into the crowd as he'd been planning, he'd tackled him and stabbed him more than a dozen times. He must have been so intent on killing the man that even unconscious, his subconscious mind had completed the mission.

"How many witnesses do they have?" Mack asked.

"They said they had one, but a friend of yours, Chris, told us there were all kinds of conflicting statements. Most of your punk rock friends are saying it was another skinhead who killed him, the guy who shot you. I guess he killed a bunch of people. He's some kind of serial killer it looks like. The cops are looking for him too. And since you'd already been shot before you attacked him, the public defender said they'd probably offer you a self-defense plea if they charged you at all, but you might still get probation for having the knife."

"If I'm on probation I can't leave the city. That means no college."

"There are plenty of colleges in Philly. Temple, Drexel, University of Penn. We'll get you into a good school. I promise."

Mack still couldn't remember anything after he tackled the short, angry-looking skinhead with the gun. He could still feel the bullets slamming into his chest and stomach, the pain when one of them shattered a bone in his arm, and his desperate attempt to stop the shooter from killing Jason. Mack remembered seeing Jason go down a second before he tackled the gunman and knocked the revolver from his hand. He remembered looking into Jason's eyes as they went vacant.

"Where's Demon? Is he alright?"

A look passed from his mother to Jonas and Mack knew. Demon was gone. He turned his head away from them so they wouldn't see the tears that welled up in his eyes. He looked out the window at the bright morning sun, blurred by his tears. Birds were singing. Cars were racing up and down the street, honking their horns in desperation to get somewhere, anywhere. Music blared from a passing vehicle with bass so loud it shook the windows. Someone walking along the sidewalk below was laughing and somewhere Demon lay dead on a slab with a tag on his toe.

"Jason died two days after you were both shot. He died on the operating table. That white supremacist shot him in the head. The doctors tried to save him, but there was nothing they could do."

"Two days? How long have I been in the hospital?"

"Three weeks."

"Three weeks?"

"You were in a coma from all the medications and pain killers and the loss of blood."

Mack sat silently, trying to take it all in.

"You said that I'm a suspect in two murders. Did the guy I beat up, the guy with the red beard, did he die?"

His mother looked puzzled.

"The cops didn't mention a guy with a red beard. They said that Jason killed that skinhead they found in the projects in Philly. His fingerprints were all over him and they think you might have been an accomplice too. They wanted to take your fingerprints, but I wouldn't let 'em. They said they were coming back today with a warrant."

Fuck.

Mack felt like he couldn't breathe. It was all over. Jason was dead, he'd missed his chance to go to college, and now he was probably going to prison for life, once they matched his fingerprints to the ones they found on Billie.

"I'm sorry, Mom. I'm sorry I—I'm sorry I let you down."

Mack wept and his mother stroked his face and tussled his Mohawk of knatty dreadlocks.

"It'll be okay. We'll get through this."

"I promised you I'd come home and …"

"Shhhh. And you did. You did come home. You're alive and that's all that matters. I was so worried. We didn't think you were going to make it, but the bullet in your chest struck just above your heart. It went straight through without hitting anything. The one in your stomach ripped up your intestines. They had to remove part of it. They said the thickness of your leather jacket and your abdominal muscles slowed the bullet down a little or else it might have gone straight through your stomach and hit your spine. You're gonna have to wear that colostomy bag for another week or two until your intestines heal, but then they say you'll be as good as new.."

Mack lifted his hospital gown. His torso was bandaged and there was a tube in his side leading to a bag of piss and shit hanging from a hook beside the bed.

"Fuck! What else can go wrong? Sorry, Mom. But this is awful. Look at me!"

176

Jonas finally spoke up.

"I told you, you shouldn't have gone out that night. You were asking for trouble. But nobody wanted to listen to me. Now what?"

Mack laughed.

"Yeah, I was waitin' for that. Good of you not to disappoint me, Jonas. What took you so long?" Mack said.

His mom whirled around and gave Jonas a look that would have cracked granite. Jonas fell silent. She turned back to Mack and ran her palm over his brow. The smoothness and warmth of her hand was the most soothing thing he could have imagined. He focused on it, trying to escape all the pain and death and misery. If he could just focus on the softness of his mother's hand, the warmth of her love, he felt like everything would be okay. It was his oasis, his happy place.

"You're lucky, son. You should feel blessed. This is only temporary. At least you're alive and you can walk. Thank God for that. He was definitely looking out for you this time."

Mack scoffed.

"Yeah, just not for Demon. I guess he only had enough power to save one of us. Or that's all he cared to save. I guess I should feel lucky that he chose to let my best friend die instead of me. Is that what I'm supposed to feel? Blessed because someone else died, because some other mother is crying instead of mine? I guess I should praise him for letting those Nazi bastards shoot me up and ruin my life?"

Mack's mother looked shocked and angry.

"Mack! Don't talk that way. I know you're angry, but Jonas is right. You could have stayed home. You didn't have to go out there. God didn't do that. That was your choice!"

Mack didn't say anything. He knew what he wanted to say. *Why did God allow those skinheads to be there anyway? Why did he create a world where pieces of shit like that exist? Why did he let them bring guns? Why didn't he make the bullets miss? He could part the red sea and murder the first born sons of Egypt and raise Lazarus from the dead, but he couldn't stop a bunch of racist white supremacist assholes from killing my best friend?*

"When is Jason's funeral?"

"I'm sorry, son. It was two weeks ago. You missed it."

"I missed it? You mean that's it? My best friend is dead and I didn't even get to say goodbye?"

"You were there, Mack. You were there in spirit, even if you couldn't be there physically. They found a poem you wrote in Jason's room. He'd framed it and put it up on a shelf. Your friend, Father Antonio, read it during the eulogy. It was beautiful. His mother found some song lyrics he wrote about you too. I don't think you ever saw them. I have 'em at the house. I'll bring it with me tomorrow. They're kind of crude. He wasn't a poet like you, but you can see how much he thought of you. He loved you so much, Mack. I'm so sorry, son. You were still unconscious from losing all that blood and the surgery. They weren't sure you didn't have brain damage. They didn't know if you were ever going to wake up."

"I knew you would."

Mack turned when he heard the voice. He recognized it immediately and it sent a chill down his spine. With all the bad news he'd heard today, this one piece of good news hit him like a splash of water.

"Miranda?"

She looked beautiful. Her head was shaved and there was a scar on her scalp from where the doctors had cut into her skull. She looked skinny. Not athletic any more, but nearly emaciated. She was wearing makeup, which was something she never did. Mack smiled when he realized that she had probably put it on for him.

She held out her hand. The engagement ring was on her finger. Mack was embarrassed by how small it was. He was embarrassed because he'd asked a girl he only kissed once to marry him and even more embarrassed because she'd never accepted his proposal. She'd lost consciousness after he gave her the ring. Now, he was in a hospital, wearing handcuffs and a colostomy bag, with the question still hanging in the air.

"I know. It was crazy. I don't know what I was thinking. We've never even been on a date. I just... I love you, Miranda. I do."

She leaned in and kissed him. It was everything he remembered.

"Yes, Mack. My answer is yes. I mean, not right now. But one day."

THIRTY

Bo's apartment, 9:45 am

The police hadn't come knocking on his door yet. That was a good sign. At least he hoped it was. Bo sat on the bed with his back to Gia, trying to decide what to do next. John Jones was dead. *The Unrest* was in shambles and somewhere Little Davey was still in hiding after murdering his ex-girlfriend and her lover and a punk rock kid he'd shot in plain view of everyone at City Gardens. If Davey got caught and confessed to killing the guy they buried in the woods or the old woman they set on fire, it would only be a matter of time before it all led back to him and Bo would be arrested as an accomplice. He had to figure something out, but so far all he could think to do was hide out in the apartment, waiting to see if the police broke down his door and dragged him off to prison.

"So, where's Little Davey now?" Gia asked. She'd been spending more and more time in the apartment with him since the riot. He told her he didn't want to go out because he'd been part of the riot and if anyone saw his bruised and battered face they'd put two and two together and try to connect him to the shooting. She knew that Davey had shot someone but she didn't yet know the extent of it. It was a few days later, when they were watching the news on his eighteen inch black and white, that the full extent of Davey's madness came out.

Little Davey was accused of killing six people, including Cindy and some guy named Alvaro that she had been sleeping with. Four of the six murders occurred while Bo had been with him. That made him an accessory and if Gia

180

found out, she'd freak out.

When Gia saw him immediately after the riot at City Gardens, she tried her best to get him to go to the hospital. But he would only allow her to call her cousin who was an EMT. Her cousin Mancini gave him some anti-inflammatories, some pain killers and ice packs and Bo spent the next few days with his head packed in ice, popping Percocets and peeking out the window for suspicious cars.

It took more than a week for the migraines to go away. It took another week for the terrible bruises all over his face to fade. The cuts and lacerations would probably take longer to disappear. Some of the scars would be with him for the rest of his life.

Bo shrugged.

"I don't know where the hell he is. He's hiding out. He probably left town. I still can't believe he killed Cindy."

Gia raised an eyebrow.

"You can't? I knew he was a little psychopath the first time I met him. I still don't understand why you're so nervous though. Why do you keep talking about leaving town if you're innocent? You sure you weren't involved in any of this? The two of you were always together. Where did you two go that night? You know, when he made you go out in the parking lot with him and you guys took off in his car? What was that all about?"

Bo kept his back to her with his head down.

"Nothing, Gia. It was nothing."

"And that black guy they found tortured and burned that they say Davey killed? You don't know nothing about that? You weren't there when he killed that guy or that old lady they say he burned alive in the subway or the guy they say he stabbed on the street a few blocks from here? You weren't with him for any of that?"

"No, Gia. I said, I don't know anything about that stuff."

Gia frowned.

"He didn't tell you he was gonna go over there and kill Cindy and her boyfriend?"

"What the fuck is this? Why are you interrogating me?"

Gia scooted across the bed and wrapped her arms around him.

"I'm just asking you the same questions the police are gonna ask. And I'm telling you, to me, you don't sound very convincing. I'm not a trained professional either. Those cops are gonna have all kinds of evidence, witnesses, and fingerprints and stuff. If you can't fool me, they're gonna rip you apart."

"That's why we should just go, get the hell out of here before they come. We could catch a train to New York or D.C. They've got too many murders there to care about us."

Gia smiled and hugged Bo tighter.

"Then what? You gonna marry me to keep me quiet?"

Bo laughed.

"Maybe. They can't force a wife to testify against her husband."

There was a loud knock on the door. Bo and Gia jumped then stared at each other, eyes wide, mouths open. A chill raced the length of Bo's spine.

"The police?" Gia asked.

"Maybe."

There was another knock. This one was even louder.

"What if it's Little Davey?"

"Then I ain't opening the door. I told you. I'm done with him."

Bo pulled on some pants and tip-toed to the door. He was just about to peek through the peephole when he heard the yell from the other side of the door.

"This is the Trenton Police Department! Open the door!"

The door exploded. Six officers in riot gear charged into the room with guns drawn.

"Don't move, you Nazi piece of shit!"

One of the officers, a slender black man in his fifties with graying hair who appeared to be the leader, a Captain or a Sergeant or something, smiled gleefully as he pointed his gun between Bo's eyes.

"Show me your hands, asshole! Your ass is goin' to death row for what you did, Beuregard or Bocephus or whatever the fuck your name is. What the fuck is Bo short for anyway?" The cop laughed.

Bo raised his hands in surrender and one the other officers tackled him. Two more police officers jumped on top of him. Their combined weight crushed the air from his lungs. It felt like they were squeezing the life from him. They rolled him over on his stomach and sat on his back. They jerked his arms behind his back so hard it felt like both shoulders dislocated as they attempted to handcuff him. Bo struggled to free himself from under them, trying to get some air.

"Don't resist! Stop resisting!" One of the police officers on his back said.

"I can't breeeeathe!" Bo wheezed.

One of the officers struck him with his baton and soon punches, kicks and batons were raining down on him. Bo felt one of the officers lodge his Billy club beneath his chin and pull. The guy was sitting on Bo's back and he was pulling so hard that he was both choking him and straining Bo's back. A gurgling sound came from his throat. He heard Gia scream.

"Let him go! You're killing him!"

Then everything went black.

EPILOGUE

Little Davey sat outside the tattoo parlor, watching two little black kids play up and down the boardwalk. They were both wet and covered in sand. They had just come up from the beach and were waiting for the boardwalk's amusement rides to open. Mickey sat in his stroller, playing with a G.I. Joe action figure. He wore tiny Doc Martin combat boots and a little, white Agnostic Front t-shirt. His head was completely shaved except for a single patch of blond hair at the very front.

"How you doin', Sport?"

Mickey looked up at his father and smiled. Davey reached down and ruffled his son's hair.

Davey remembered talking with Skinner once about the Atlanta Child Murders and how that guy had the right idea. *Killing little black kids would fill the entire race with mortal terror of the white man... as it should be*, he thought.

"Hey buddy, you're up."

Little Davey stood up and walked inside the tiny tattoo shop. It was just barely larger than a walk-in closet. There was only one chair, a barber's chair. There were pictures of tattoos all over the walls. The big bald guy who owned the place had a confederate flag tattooed on his neck along with an iron cross on the back of his hand and a plethora of other tattoos in between, mostly skulls, heavy metal lyrics, and naked women. That's why Davey chose this filthy rundown tattoo parlor among all the other tattoo shops on the boardwalk. He looked like the kind of guy who could relate to Davey's cause.

"My name's Hank," the big bald guy said. He didn't offer to shake hands.

"David. Pleased to meet you, brother."

Hank nodded toward Davey's son.

"Cute kid. So what do you want?"

Davey climbed into the seat and rolled up his sleeve. He handed Hank a piece of paper.

"I want this, in two inch gothic lettering, all the way up my arm."

"You want this symbol too?" Hank asked.

"Oh yes. Absolutely," Davey replied.

Hank shrugged.

"You're the customer."

Davey was in the chair for five hours. Hank, played *Slayer, White Snake* and *Hank William's Jr.* on a stereo set up by the front door while he inked the big letters on Davey's skin from the inside of his elbow to his wrist. When he was done, Davey stood up and admired the design in the mirror.

There was a swastika tattooed on his wrist and another in the crook of his arm. In between, in big, two-inch gothic lettering, just as he'd requested, were the words "The Unrest Lives!"

"Beautiful. You do good work."

"Yeah, thanks. That'll be two hundred dollars."

"Take a check?"

"Fuck no!"

"I'm just kidding. Here you go." Davey counted out two hundred dollars in twenties and handed it to Hank. Hank grimaced.

"Is that blood?"

The twenties had turned brown, stained with old blood. Davey smiled.

"Does it matter?"

Hank scowled.

"I hope these ain't marked bills. I don't need that kind of trouble."

"I didn't rob a bank if that's what you mean."

Hank eyed him suspiciously then nodded his head and shoved the brownish red bills into the cash register.

"Okay. You have a nice day." He held the door open and Davey stepped out into the sunlight, pushing the stroller ahead of him. Spring was just a few weeks away and it was going to be a glorious one.

"You might want to put some Neosporin on that. And don't scratch or you'll fuck it all up. Good luck."

Davey smiled.

"Thanks, Hank."

He looked down the boardwalk, searching for the two black kids he'd seen playing earlier. It was still early and the boardwalk was mostly empty. The rides had just opened and a small line was beginning to form for the rollercoaster. He spotted the two kids a block away, heading toward the Ferris wheel. Their parents were nowhere in sight.

Little Davey reached into his pocket and gripped the hilt of his new bowie knife as he started down the boardwalk with his son. He leaned down and whispered in Mickey's ear.

"You're about to learn a valuable lesson today son, how to deal with the lesser races. They need to be put in their place. You watch, daddy will show you."

There were lots of dark isolated places once you got off the boardwalk. There were alleys and side streets where nobody ever went. It might take a few hours, but eventually he knew they'd leave the boardwalk and he'd be right behind them. He looked down at his new tattoo and smiled, feeling that old excitement and anticipation, that rush of adrenalin.

The Unrest lives. He thought. *The Unrest Lives!*

DEMON CHILD
BY
MAXWELL "MACK" JOHNSON

Some demons haunt our nightmares
Others inspire us to dream
to mischief and sin
dark music and pleasure
violent combat and dance
Some demons embarrass us
And some amuse us.
My demon child is a wild thing
Full of fire and love
He makes me forget my pain
Makes me feel invincible
Makes me laugh when I should cry
Makes me live when I want to die
My demon child is a crazy thing
Full of rage and joy
He fights for me
and I for him
He'd die for me
And I for him
He lives for me
And I for him
My demon child
is my best friend.

UNSTOPPABLE
BY
JASON "DEMON" SADLER

You can't stop him when he's rollin'
Runnin' down skins like an eighteen wheeler
When he's runnin' or he's strollin'
Racists all flee from the black death dealer!

Unstoppable!
Like a Mack truck
Irresistible!
Like a Mack truck
Runnin' 'em down!
Runnin' 'em down!
Runnin' 'em down!
He's runnin' 'em down!

When he's on the scene
Stompin' through the pit in his big black boots
He's a moshin' machine
Stompin' on skins with his big black boots

Unstoppable!
Like a Mack truck
Irresistible!
Like a Mack truck
Runnin' 'em down!
Runnin' 'em down!
Runnin' 'em down!
He's runnin' 'em down!

WRATH JAMES WHITE is the author of *The Resurrectionist, Succulent Prey, Yacob's Curse, Sacrifice, Pure Hate,* and *Prey Drive (Succulent Prey Part II)*. He is also the author of *Voracious, To The Death, Skinzz, The Reaper, Like Porno for Psychos, Everyone Dies Famous In A Small Town, The Book of a Thousand Sins, His Pain,* and *Population Zero*. He is the co-author of *Teratologist* co-written with the king of extreme horror, Edward Lee, *Orgy of Souls* co-written with Maurice Broaddus, *The Killings* and *Hero* co-written with J.F. Gonzalez, *Son of a Bitch* co-written with Andre Duza and *Poisoning Eros I and II* co-written with Monica J. O'Rourke.

His short stories have appeared in several dozen magazines and anthologies. In 2010, his poetry collection, *Vicious Romantic* was nominated for a Bram Stoker Award.

deadite press

"Header" Edward Lee - In the dark backwoods, where law enforcement doesn't dare tread, there exists a special type of revenge. Something so awful that it is only whispered about. Something so terrible that few believe it is real. Stewart Cummings is a government agent whose life is going to Hell. His wife is ill and to pay for her medication he turns to bootlegging. But things will get much worse when bodies begin showing up in his sleepy small town. Victims of an act known only as "a Header."

"Entombed II" Brian Keene- It has been several months since the disease known as Hamelin's Revenge decimated the world. Civilization has collapsed and the dead far outnumber the living. The survivors seek refuge from the roaming zombie hordes, but one-by-one, those shelters are falling. Twenty-five survivors barricade themselves inside a former military bunker buried deep beneath a luxury hotel. They are safe from the zombies...but are they safe from one another?

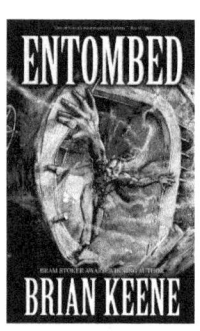

"Zombies and Shit" Carlton Mellick III - Twenty people wake to find themselves in a boarded-up building in the middle of the zombie wasteland. They soon discover they have been chosen as contestants on a popular reality show called Zombie Survival. Each contestant is given a backpack of supplies and a unique weapon. Their goal: be the first to make it through the zombie-plagued city to the pick-up zone alive. But because there's only one seat available on the helicopter, the contestants not only have to fight against the hordes of the living dead, they must also fight each other.

"Muerte Con Carne" Shane McKenzie - Human flesh tacos, hardcore wrestling, and angry cannibal Mexicans, Welcome to the Border! Felix and Marta came to Mexico to film a documentary on illegal immigration. When Marta suddenly goes missing, Felix must find his lost love in the small border town. A dangerous place housing corrupt cops, borderline maniacs, and something much more worse than drug gangs, something to do with a strange Mexican food cart...

deadite press

"Urban Gothic" Brian Keene - When their car broke down in a dangerous inner-city neighborhood, Kerri and her friends thought they would find shelter inside an old, dark row home. They thought they would be safe there until help arrived. They were wrong. The residents who live down in the cellar and the tunnels beneath the city are far more dangerous than the streets outside, and they have a very special way of dealing with trespassers. Trapped in a world of darkness, populated by obscene abominations, they will have to fight back if they ever want to see the sun again.

"Ghoul" Brian Keene - There is something in the local cemetery that comes out at night. Something that is unearthing corpses and killing people. It's the summer of 1984 and Timmy and his friends are looking forward to no school, comic books, and adventure. But instead they will be fighting for their lives. The ghoul has smelled their blood and it is after them. But that's not the only monster they will face this summer . . . From award-winning horror master Brian Keene comes a novel of monsters, murder, and the loss of innocence.

"Clickers" J. F. Gonzalez and Mark Williams- They are the Clickers, giant venomous blood-thirsty crabs from the depths of the sea. The only warning to their rampage of dismemberment and death is the terrible clicking of their claws. But these monsters aren't merely here to ravage and pillage. They are being driven onto land by fear. Something is hunting the Clickers. Something ancient and without mercy. *Clickers* is J. F. Gonzalez and Mark Williams' gore-soaked cult classic tribute to the giant monster B-movies of yesteryear.

"Clickers II" J. F. Gonzalez and Brian Keene- Thousands of Clickers swarm across the entire nation and march inland, slaughtering anyone and anything they come across. But this time the Clickers aren't blindly rushing onto land - they are being led by an intelligence older than civilization itself. A force that wants to take dry land away from the mammals. Those left alive soon realize that they must do everything and anything they can to protect humanity – no matter the cost. *This isn't war; this is extermination.*

"The Book of a Thousand Sins" Wrath James White - Welcome to a world of Zombie nymphomaniacs, psychopathic deities, voodoo surgery, and murderous priests. Where mutilation sex clubs are in vogue and torture machines are sex toys. No one makes it out alive – not even God himself.
"If Wrath James White doesn't make you cringe, you must be riding in the wrong end of a hearse."
    -Jack Ketchum

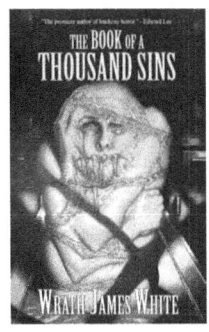

"Whargoul" Dave Brockie - It is a beast born in bullets and shrapnel, feeding off of pain, misery, and hard drugs. Cursed to wander the Earth without the hope of death, it is reborn again and again to spread the gospel of hate, abuse, and genocide. But what if it's not the only monster out there? What if there's something worse? From Dave Brockie, the twisted genius behind GWAR, comes a novel about the darkest days of the twentieth century.

"Take the Long Way Home" Brian Keene - All across the world, people suddenly vanish in the blink of an eye. Gone. Steve, Charlie and Frank were just trying to get home when it happened. Trapped in the ultimate traffic jam, they watch as civilization collapses, claiming the souls of those around them. God has called his faithful home, but the invitations for Steve, Charlie and Frank got lost. Now they must set off on foot through a nightmarish post-apocalyptic landscape in search of answers. In search of God. In search of their loved ones. And in search of home.

"Baby's First Book of Seriously Fucked-Up Shit" Robert Devereaux - From an orgy between God, Satan, Adam and Eve to beauty pageants for fetuses. From a giant human-absorbing tongue to a place where God is in the eyes of the psychopathic. This is a party at the furthest limits of human decency and cruelty. Robert Devereaux is your host but watch out, he's spiked the punch with drugs, sex, and dismemberment. Deadite Press is proud to present nine stories of the strange, the gross, and the just plain fucked up.

THE VERY BEST IN CULT HORROR